RESTLESS NATIVES

NINIAN DUNNETT

Restless Natives

CHATTO & WINDUS

THE HOGARTH PRESS
LONDON

Published in 1985 by
Chatto & Windus · The Hogarth Press
40 William IV Street
London WC2N 4DF

British Library Cataloguing in Publication Data

Dunnett, Ninian
Restless natives.
I. Title
823′914[F]   PR6054.U5/

ISBN 0 7011 3954 4
ISBN 0 7011 3955 2 Pbk

Restless Natives
is an Oxford Film Company Production
in association with THORN EMI Screen Entertainment,
screenplay by Ninian Dunnett,
music by Big Country,
produced by Rick Stevenson
and directed by Michael Hoffman.

Typeset by Rowland Phototypesetting Ltd
Bury St Edmunds, Suffolk
Printed in Great Britain by
Redwood Burn Ltd,
Trowbridge, Wiltshire

For my father

— I —

That smell. It started to seep around Will's nose as soon as he tried the helmet on. There was no other smell like it. Will whipped off the helmet and threw it down on his bed. What was he going to tell Ronnie?

Time was getting on. Will started jamming on his jeans and stopped after one leg, trying to remember if Ronnie had said anything about clothes. Just jeans and jackets, he thought. His head was still fuddled with sleep, and he guided himself by hand through the short dark corridor to the kitchen, trying to make as little noise as possible, the empty leg of the jeans trailing after him.

Sitting by the kitchen table, he pulled on the rest of the jeans and stared through the window. The dark blue sky outside was beginning to outline the other tower blocks on the estate. Father was still fast asleep. He was probably snoring, right now. Will shuffled back up the corridor and leaned his head to the main bedroom door. Yes, snoring.

Back in the kitchen Will pasted up several jeely pieces, drinking a glass of water as he worked. He hadn't been able to get to sleep until after two for thinking about today, but he was still up long before Father.

Time was getting on. He packed the sandwiches into a plastic carrier-bag and crammed them into his Army and Navy Stores satchel. Then he went back up the corridor and stood by the front door of the flat, waiting.

He seemed to wait a long time. He stood listening to the muffled noise from his parents' room. It wasn't a bad snore, really, certainly a mature snore. It didn't have any of the whistling or sudden snorts or muttering of a totally unpleasant snore. It was a tuneful, consistent snore.

A tap at the outside door made Will jump. He whispered through the lock. 'Ronnie?'

'Open up, ya bam.'

Will unlocked the door. Ronnie was wearing his helmet, looking up at Will through his glasses under the raised visor. He had the sort of glasses that had a blue tinge in them, though he never said why. Ronnie was getting impatient.

'Ready?'

'Shh. Aye.'

Ronnie gestured to Will's satchel. 'What's that?'

Will was pleased with himself. It was going to be a nice day. 'Jeely piece. Apricot jam.'

'Got your helmet?'

'Oh Christ.'

'What?'

'Shh Ronnie.' Will ran back to his bedroom and fetched the helmet. On his way to the door he took a quick sniff. Just as bad. Oh Christ. He held it up to Ronnie.

'Cat's peed in it.'

Ronnie backed off angrily.

'What? Ma second best helmet?'

'Shh Ronnie. I couldnae help it. It was in the hall. It's her bladder, ye know.'

'Come on, bring it and shut the door.'

They took the steps for the eight floors down to the ground, with Ronnie doing most of the talking. Will was worrying about the cat's bladder. She was getting old and creaky, and he wondered about nappies.

'I thought ye were gonnae look after it. Ye cannae take that lining out, ye know, ye'll have tae soak it, it'll probably never be the same.'

'Aye. I'm sorry. But – what about now?'

Ronnie fixed his blue-tinted lenses on Will.

'Well ye'll have tae wear it, won't ye?'

As they emerged at ground level Will squeezed the helmet back on his head, sticking his nose out of the open visor as far as possible to try and take in the early morning air. He fiddled with the strap under his chin, but he couldn't tighten it. The helmet was too tight and the strap was too loose. Did Ronnie have a small

2

head and a big chin? Will peered at him, trying to judge from what he could see of Ronnie under his visor. They had reached the bike, parked beside the pavement.

'Ronnie.'

Ronnie turned and fiddled with Will's helmet impatiently, tightening the strap and making a face as he caught a whiff of its contents.

'That's terrible, that is. Come on, ye big bairn.'

Ronnie mounted the bike and tried the starter. It fired on the third kick. Will got on the back, gripping the strap on the seat tightly and wishing they would get moving and clear the acid cloud that seemed to be settling round his head. Ronnie gunned the engine, and then shot off with a speed that strained Will's grip to the limit. Four G's, he thought to himself, imagining his face muscles rippling with the pressure as the bike roared away.

Dawn had chased the night from the city. The bike rattled through the tree-lined streets of the suburbs, startling a stumbling drunk on his way home.

At Redford Barracks the distant rasp of its engine mingled with the reveille, and Maori dancers, the Pipes and Drums of the Argyll and Sutherland Highlanders, a unit of the South Eastern Fire Brigade and the band of the Isle of Barbados Police Force began their day's preparations for the Edinburgh Military Tattoo.

On Lothian Road the lone motorbike became a talking-point for the first wave of the morning's army of cleaners, chattering in the bus on their way to their nylon coats and mops in a hundred factories and offices.

Festive flags stirred briefly in its wake along the city's main thoroughfare, Princes Street. A gaggle of tourists emerging on to the road from the London sleeper train stopped to let it go by.

A milk-horse pulling a laden cart down the cobbled streets of the New Town snorted at its clatter.

Litter blew about beneath its wheels as it headed on northwards towards the coast, and children wandering to school stopped to stare.

At the shoreline where the great road bridge spans the Firth of Forth, its shadow slipped quietly across the glinting water for a mile and then into Fife.

Will was enjoying the ride. Ronnie drove fast, and the wind lashed mercifully through the open visor of Will's helmet, filling his face with fresh air.

The morning traffic was just starting to appear on the motorway when Ronnie turned off on to an older road, and the bike raced between lines of trees, hedges and dry-stone dykes, seeming to go faster than ever.

In the distance across the hilly farmland came the first mountains of the Highlands, solid and wild-looking above the tame countryside. Soon the bike was among them, racing with a river on a twisting valley road. A gang of rocky giants gathered above Will and Ronnie where there had just been sky before.

Will rubbed his eyes as Ronnie slowed the bike and pulled into a grassy clearing by the road. Ronnie fished a crumpled mess of paper from a zip pocket in his leather jacket, and carefully flattened it out into a single sheet. It was a map. Will peered over Ronnie's shoulder.

'Where we going?'

Ronnie craned round to look at him. 'I don't know where we're going. It disnae matter where we're going. We've just got tae find the right spot.' He craned round further to give Will a long-suffering stare. 'But if we dinnae know where we get tae, we won't know how tae get back, will we?'

Ronnie returned to the map, tracing his finger unsurely across it as Will watched him. There was something familiar about it.

'Where's that frae?' Will asked.

'School atlas.' Ronnie stopped puzzling at the map, apparently satisfied, and crumpling it up again he stashed it back in his pocket and pulled out a chewed-up ballpoint pen.

'B9366,' he said importantly, writing it on the back of his hand. Will poked into his satchel, and pulled out his plastic carrier-bag. Ronnie turned to gaze at him again.

'Whit ye doin'?'

'Jeely piece,' said Will happily, pulling out one of the oozing yellow and white lumps.

'This isnae a picnic, ye know,' Ronnie shouted. 'This is serious. This has got tae be done properly.' He watched as Will stuffed the sandwiches back into the satchel, and then he started the bike and pushed it full throttle off down the single-track road.

Will didn't mind not having his piece. He was quite happy to have the wind whistling through his face again. The hills seemed to be getting bigger around them as the bike travelled further north, and the heather was out, he could see the purple.

The road passed along the very edge of a loch, and all the hills and trees were doubled by the clear sun in the water. Where the rock rose in a cliff on the other side of the road a long waterfall splashed down. Will wondered why he'd never come here before.

When the road crossed the brow of a gentle, dome-shaped hill, Ronnie brought the bike to a halt at the top, and he and Will surveyed the land. They seemed to be very high up, and a gentle breeze tickled around them. Looking back down the road Will could see the peaks and ridges descending to a distant loch which shimmered silver in the sun. The hill they were on sloped down on either side to a valley, but on the far side of both valleys mountains rose to rocky summits above the road. They were almost at the top of the world.

'This'll do,' said Ronnie.

At the brow of the hill Ronnie parked the bike on its stand half-way across the road. Will tried to undo the strap of his helmet.

'No, ye'll have tae keep it on,' Ronnie said.

Will stammered, 'Ye don't know what it's like –'

'Ye'll have tae keep it on. We dinnae have any choice.'

Will sat down on the grass at the edge of the road. Ronnie paced up and down impatiently.

The sun beamed down on Will's gleaming black helmet. In the padded interior of the plastic shell, complex chemical reactions were taking place. Many minutes went by, and suddenly Will jumped up, running like a madman.

He ran as fast as his skinny legs could go, away off down the road, and by the time Ronnie yelled after him he had already turned round and was flapping furiously back. He sprinted straight past Ronnie and off in the other direction, and then turned again, flailing like a crazed bird.

Ronnie's face had gone very white, but none of his shouting or screaming made the slightest bit of difference. He watched Will flutter past three times before he staggered and collapsed full-length at Ronnie's feet.

'Had tae get some air,' Will gasped. 'Had tae. Sorry. Ye don't know what it's like.'

'And whit d'ye suppose would have happened if somebody had came along while you were in the middle of yer act?' Ronnie shouted, but leaning over Will he wrinkled his nose suddenly and left it at that.

It was getting near lunchtime, but Will had no appetite. He sat at the side of the road, trying to forget the sandwiches in his satchel. Ronnie paced.

There was a noise in the distance. Will stood up and looked at Ronnie, whose head was tilted to one side. A car.

'Close your visor!' said Ronnie, and Will did. Ronnie lowered the visor on his own helmet. It was the expensive, mirrored type. Several hundred yards down the road, a dirty yellow car appeared. Ronnie stood in the middle of the road, his arm raised in a traffic policeman's 'halt' position, and Will watched the car drive slowly up and stop.

A middle-aged, red-faced woman with permed hair wound down her passenger-seat window, and peered up at Ronnie. She looked cross. In the back of the car sat a little girl chewing gum, stretching it in long strings from her mouth, and a little boy humming to himself. They both stared as Ronnie bent over to speak through the window.

A muffled, mumbling sound echoed inside his helmet. The woman spoke impatiently.

'I beg your pardon?'

Carefully Ronnie raised his visor to about the level of his nose before he spoke again.

'This is a hold up. Hand over all your money and –'

'Oh,' the woman's groan interrupted him. She turned bad-temperedly to her husband.

'Rag Week.'

She dug fussily into her handbag and then her purse. A balding man in the driver's seat leaned over towards the open window where Ronnie stood motionless.

'What's that?' the man asked.

'Students,' grunted his wife without glancing up. She pulled a fifty-pence piece out of her purse and held it out to Ronnie. Ronnie took it without a word.

'There you are,' she said. 'And don't waste your breath asking for any more, you're the third this week already.'

'Hey Jim,' the driver shouted up to Ronnie, 'd'ye know if we're on the right road for Inverlochy?'

'Just drive on, Alex,' Ronnie heard the woman say to her husband. 'They live in a world of their own, these kids.'

The car shifted into gear and quietly skirted round Ronnie's bike as the woman wound up her window. The little girl was staring at him through the back window of the car. Very slowly she raised her hand in a V-sign.

'Ronnie. Ronnie.'

Ronnie turned. Will was standing at the side of the road. He had lifted his steamed-up visor, and his face was all sweating and horrible. Black streaks ran down his cheeks where the dye of the helmet fabric had dissolved with sweat. He was shaking his head, trying to catch some outside air through the front of the helmet. His hands tore at the strap under his chin.

'Please,' he gasped. 'Please. Help me.'

It hadn't been a great day, Will decided. A good day, but not a great one. The few minutes where his head had been stuck in the helmet with the visor down, drowning in that terrible heat and taste and smell – that wasn't much fun. But it didn't sound as if he'd missed much, and once they were back on the bike he was fine, and even managed to eat his jeely pieces while they were going.

If they'd found their way home all right there wouldn't have been much to complain about. Ronnie said it was the launderette's fault, because the machines always did 'hot wash' when you set them to 'warm wash' and it was 'hot wash' that made everything in your pockets fall apart, which was why the map had been so blurry on the bit where he thought it said B9366.

Will had to keep telling Ronnie that in some ways it had been quite a successful expedition. But while he was soaking the helmet in hot water and watching all the black dye come out and realised the lining was disintegrating, another thought occurred to him. If the expedition had been completely successful, he would now be a criminal. The more he thought about it, the more it worried him.

Also the cat had been sick while he was away, and he felt responsible.

So by the time he went in to the Joke Shop to see Ronnie on Monday morning, he had mixed feelings about the day, and however hard he tried, he couldn't unmix them.

'I'm no saying it's a complete failure, I'm no saying that,' he said, leaning on the counter.

Ronnie was standing behind the glass-topped counter, arranging a pile of different-coloured rubber insects into several tiny cardboard boxes. He didn't look as if he was listening, but there weren't any customers in the shop, and Will wanted to sort this out.

'I'm no bothered about that,' Will said, 'I'm just saying that maybe it's no right, that sort o' thing.'

He watched Ronnie hopefully, but as Ronnie looked up a little girl in a checked dress marched through the shop door and up to the counter, where she whispered something in Ronnie's ear. Ronnie leaned behind him to the great racks of wooden drawers, pulled something out of one of them, and placed it on the counter. It was a plastic turd. The little girl handed over some change, picked the thing up, and marched out. Will tried again as Ronnie worked the cash register.

'I mean, don't ye think in some ways it's a bad thing just tae take other people's money? It is. People work hard for their money, some o' them.'

Ronnie glanced up doubtfully from the rubber insects, and Will had another idea. It was important to make Ronnie understand.

'And what if the police find out? Have you any idea how much it costs just tae send one policeman out on a case? There's petrol, wear and tear, expenses, overtime – that's taxpayers' money, ye know.'

Ronnie looked as if he was going to say something now, but through the shop door came a boy in short trousers, with a very dirty face. He held up a little scrap of paper and started to read: 'Stink bomb, bangers, nasty sugar . . .'

Ronnie hurriedly grubbed into the drawers and boxes around and behind the counter to get each item on the shopping list, and then turned back to the boy, frowning.

'You sure about the nasty sugar?'

The boy seemed sure. 'Aye. Three packs.' He turned back to his list, '. . . dried worms, fake scab, black soap.'

As Ronnie put the last item on the counter the boy heaved a huge mound of change from his pocket on to the glass top, turning his pocket out to get the last pennies. Will watched him admiringly as he gathered up the haul and strode out of the shop. Then Ronnie leaned across the counter as if he was going to whisper something.

9

'Whit do you want out o' life?'

This wasn't what Will had expected, but he started to give it some thought. Ronnie took a spring-loaded toy from under the counter and set it up in front of Will. Will began to speak.

'Well –'

'Ye want excitement,' Ronnie said decisively, and as the jump-bug leapt into the air in front of Will's face Ronnie caught it without blinking. Very classy. But Will wasn't sure he had got his message across.

'No, I think –'

'And ye want money, right?' Ronnie said. Will didn't answer. His left hand felt sort of itchy. He could see Ronnie was starting to enjoy this conversation. Ronnie caught the jump-bug in mid-air again as he carried on, 'Because without money, ye cannae dae anything.'

Now Ronnie leaned even further over the counter. Will couldn't decide whether to look at Ronnie, whose face was only a few inches away, or at his own left hand, which had begun to worry him. Ronnie's eyes seemed bigger than usual through his blue-tinted lenses as he carried on.

'Listen. You and yer bad things. It's a bad thing I'm sellin' jump-bugs and you're on the corporation. It's a bad thing tae settle for a little when you can get a lot out of life. The point is, we're smarter than they are.'

Ronnie waved his arm importantly towards the shop door. But Will had other things to think about. Something terrible had happened.

Will didn't expect Ronnie to understand about his hand. He showed it to him, of course, but Ronnie didn't say a word. For the rest of the day Will tried to forget about it, thinking they might go away, but he kept remembering there was something he had to forget. On the bus home he looked again, very closely, and they seemed to be bigger. There were five, two on the insides of fingers, one just above a big dip in either his love-line or his life-line, and two on the back.

There were two little girls sitting behind him, and he tuned in to their high-pitched conversation.

'Did ye see yon zombie flesh one?'

'Aye that was great.'

'The bit where he comes in and she's all on fire and he cuts her up the middle?'

'Aye that was great.'

Will hadn't been to church since he gave up Sunday School at the age of nine, but there was a phrase he couldn't get out of his mind: 'the wages of sin'. He looked at his hand again. 'A plague of boils', he thought, but these looked more like warts. Maybe he could take to wearing a glove, like the Phantom of the Opera.

At tea Will wanted to ask about the warts, but he was embarrassed, and ended up complaining about his work, and this set Father off. Father thought he could do great impersonations of his family, and once the idea got into his head he could go on for hours.

'There jist doesnae seem tae be any point tae it all,' he whined, screwing his face up and tilting his head to one side. Will knew he didn't sound or look anything like that.

Father went back to his normal face. 'Oh Mary I cannae stand the strain,' he said. 'First of all he gets a job, and now the boy's turning intae a deep thinker. What next, son? A nation waits.'

Will had a forkful of steak and kidney pie in his mouth, and struggled to swallow it so he could say something to Father's questioning stare. Mother spoke.

'He knows he's lucky tae have a job, don't you dear?' she said briskly. 'He's jist tired and he wants tae eat his food.' She shovelled another forkful of pie into her own mouth.

Isla said, 'Carol Paton's big brother's gone tae New Mexico.' Will's sister was only twelve, but she had perfected the technique of eating without chewing, and this left her free for conversation. She looked innocently at Will. 'And he's going tae be earning five hundred pounds a week.'

Will didn't know Carol Paton's big brother, but Will could picture him, a snooty twit in a sta-press three-piece suit, wart-free. Will glared at Isla, who looked dreamily past him. Father went on, spattering little gobbets of steak and kidney back on to the plate in front of him.

'Aye, there's opportunities for them that wants them.' He stopped chewing, leaning over sarcastically towards Will. 'What's the matter, son? It's his biorhythms, he cannae help himsel'.'

Will surrendered, bowing his head as he ate. Last summer he had read a thing in the newspaper on biorhythms, the secret inner clocks that control your well-being. He'd even started to draw up a chart for himself so he could tell what days all three of his bio-lines were at low ebb and avoid disasters by staying in bed. Isla found the chart and told Father.

There was silence at the table for a few seconds.

'Mum, can I go down the disco Saturday?' Isla asked sweetly.

Mother started stacking the empty plates and looked tired. 'What time does it finish?'

'Ten thirty, I think.'

Will gave Isla a long stare. Isla ignored it. Mother took the dishes to the sink.

'Ask your father, Isla,' Mother said. Father couldn't miss a cue like that.

'That's too late a thing for you, young lady,' Father said, 'so ye can jist put it right out of your mind.'

Isla switched tactics straight away. 'Mum, Annie White's going, and I said I'd promise to go with her, and all my pals will be there, and it's not really late you know.'

Mother was filling the sink, and spoke without turning round. 'We'll think about it, okay?' Isla nodded glumly, and silence fell.

This was Will's chance. Now or never. 'Mum,' he said. She still didn't turn round. No going back. 'Does doing bad things give ye warts?'

Mother turned round. Everyone was looking at Will strangely. He grinned, hoping that might help. Mother turned back to the sink. Will tried as casually as possible to slide his hands off the table, and sat on them.

'I think that's somethin' ye'd better discuss with your father later, Will,' Mother said. Now Father was looking at Mother strangely. Isla giggled. What was happening?

Isla said, 'Maybe if I stayed at Annie White's I'd be able to get back earlier.' Mother gave Isla an evil glare. Father leaned forward on the table, stared grimly at Will, and began to speak.

'When I was your age ye had tae see the doctor for yer warts, and he'd burn them off for ye.' Father was beginning to enjoy himself. Will squirmed in his seat. 'You'd lie on the couch, and the great fat nurse would paint red ointment on to each wart.' Father painted his own hand precisely with an imaginary paintbrush, grinning up at Will, who gripped his hands tightly together. Father went on. 'Oh, the stench wis somethin' terrible. Then he'd get his great long needle, white-hot like a poker it was, an' the nurse held ye down, oh you were screaming then –' Will held back a scream. Father was waving the imaginary white-hot needle over his own hand. 'And he'd poke the needle right at ye, closer and closer, till suddenly TSSSSSSSSSS! Right intae the root! TSSSSSSSSSS!'

He was lucky to have a job, he kept telling himself. It was a city council scheme, apprenticeships on the council staff, which for Will meant a thirty-hour week clearing rubbish from public parks. The best thing about it was that, although he often worked in the evenings after the parks were closed, he never started before ten in the morning. Father just couldn't understand that.

But it was difficult to forget the £4.75 extra he'd be getting on the dole if he didn't have a job at all. Normally, if it wasn't for unemployment and council schemes, there wouldn't be anyone clearing up the rubbish during the day, especially in the busy parks. It was like trying to dry up a river by baling it out at the bottom. Most of all in Princes Street Gardens, where he was working on this day.

The gardens were very beautiful, carefully laid out in the valley between the cliff rock of the castle and Princes Street itself. Trees and flowers of all colours were set out around the central walkway, and the floral clock at the east end, the concerts in the bandstand,

and the piazza café at the west end brought loads of tourists in from the main street to mix with locals taking a short cut or heading for an empty spot of grass to sunbathe.

Will had long since realised that every attraction in the garden was a curse that brought the population of the world to bury him under its rubbish. When he had applied for the Gardens shift he was surprised no one else wanted to spend their working days in such a place, and wondered why the other dole-dodgers sniggered knowingly; but he didn't wonder any more. The noise of the bandstand concerts hurt his ears, the sight of every tree and flower was a horror to his eyes, and his friendship with Eddie the man in the ice cream van died the death as soon as he understood the connection between Eddie and some of his most horrible cleaning-up jobs.

Sometimes when things got too much Will would sneak past surprised lovers through a fence in the bushes at the bottom of the gardens and sit at the edge of the railway line which ran directly under Castle Rock, imagining taking a train somewhere exciting.

On sunny days the paths through the gardens were like motor-ways with people charging through shedding trash, and Will felt like a lone pedestrian. He would sweep a small stretch where there was a pause in the traffic, dancing round in a semi-circle to collect the rubbish into a pile behind him, and then turn round to find that his work in the road had diverted the traffic straight through his pile, scattering it.

At first Will was amazed at what people would leave in the park. Not just food of every sort and its wrappings, or ordinary paper and tissues and string and magazines and batteries and combs and empty bottles and cans, but photographs of themselves, empty shopping-bags, and strangest of all, clothing – especially under-wear, shoes and socks. Will had never seen anyone leave the park barefoot or naked.

But his interest in the booty faded very quickly, and even when he found coins now or the occasional pound note he automatically threw them straight into the bin on his yellow trolley.

Warts or no warts this was not a good day. The sun brought

14

crowds through the gardens, and a gusty wind was helping to scatter their litter far and wide. Will concentrated on trying to keep the path clear, running across it through breaks in the traffic to fetch particularly colourful scraps, only to get back to his pile and see that new ones had replaced them on the thoroughfare.

Two young Mods in pork-pie hats ran straight through his first pile, kicking most of it across the grass. Half an hour later he had remade the pile, and found a pair of fat American tourists standing right on it, taking pictures of the castle. They wouldn't move, though he tugged at the rubbish under them.

A small boy in dungarees came past with a double strawberry-flavour cone from Eddie's van, balancing the top-heavy structure unsteadily. The ice cream slowly toppled, slithered off the boy's dungarees and glouped on to the dusty ground. Will took his shovel from the trolley and headed for the mess, but as he got near the boy leaned down and scooped up the bulk of the ice cream in his hand, stuck it back into the cone, and began to lick happily at it. From the safety of his pile Will saw the boy's mother whack the boy across the head with a force which sent the ice cream, cone and all, spinning to the ground again.

Will headed for the mess with his shovel, watching it slowly smear across the path under passing feet. Five minutes later he was walking back to the pile with the remains when a gust of wind blew down the sunny valley. Will stopped and watched as his pile of rubbish floated up into the air and fell back piece by piece over the grass.

Will hadn't planned to quit his job that day. As he slowly unbuttoned and took off his overalls he still wasn't fully conscious of what he was doing. There was no accounting for it. He crumpled up the overalls and put them in the trolley with his brush and shovel. Then he walked across the road, past the bus-stop, to Waverley Station, where he bought a twenty-five pence ticket and caught the next slow train to Glasgow.

He left the train at Slateford Station, and walked the last two miles to Wester Hailes.

− 3 −

Ronnie and Bruce had been best pals for just over a year. In fact, they had moved into the bedsit together last summer, and Ronnie had been very glad of the company through those first days in his new home. For a long time he'd lived alone or with people who didn't understand him, but Bruce was different.

One day about three weeks after moving in, Bruce wouldn't get out of bed to eat his breakfast. Ronnie poked and prodded at him, getting more and more worried, and finally just pulled all his bedding off. Bruce had had two babies. It was a hell of a shock.

The old man at the pet shop said he was very sorry, he didn't know how he could have made the mistake, because it was easy to tell with hamsters. Back in the bedsit Ronnie held Bruce up to the light with one hand, and held his *Make The Most Of Your Hamster* book in the other, but the diagrams weren't anything like real life. Bruce certainly looked a lot thinner and fitter than before.

The man at the pet shop offered to do a swap for Bruce, but Ronnie couldn't do that. Anyway the man said it would never happen again. Will's sister's friend Mary Harrison gave Ronnie twenty pence each for the baby hamsters once their eyes opened, and everything was back to normal. Ronnie could never have afforded to feed three mouths. Bruce took it all in his stride.

Ronnie's home was Bruce's home, and whenever Ronnie was in, Bruce was allowed to wander about the bedsit and do just what he liked. If there had been a hamster Everest, Bruce would have been the hamster Edmund Hilary. He could go straight up the back of the wardrobe and climb into Ronnie's suitcase on top.

Bruce knew the bedsit like the back of his hand, and it was getting harder and harder for Ronnie to play Hunt the Sunflower Seed with him. Ronnie tried taking him out on the bike for a quick run up the motorway to broaden his horizons, but it didn't go down well. Bruce huddled in a jacket pocket all the way, except for once when he nearly jumped under the wheels of an articulated lorry.

On the first Saturday of every month Bruce and his cage disappeared into the wardrobe for three hours while Mrs Denzler came for her monthly inspection and rent collection. She always complained about the mess on the floor, but she was ignorant. Mrs Denzler wouldn't know a hamster shit if it hit her in the eye.

The night after Will gave up his job, Ronnie was sitting by the window, giving an interview. The sunlight was fading to a gentle glow outside and Ronnie felt fine, leaning back in his chair with his legs crossed. He took a long drag at his cigarette, flicked the ash out of the window and blew a careful funnel of smoke at the ceiling before he spoke.

'Yes, well I suppose ye could say I got intae crime as somethin' of an accident,' he said.

Outside, a lorry clattered by, and pretty girls in twos and threes strolled across the road to dance classes in the church hall. Ronnie knew that all this was going on, and he liked it. This was life. He took off his glasses and waved them dramatically in the air, staring levelly at the interviewer on the other side of the room.

'The thing in life is tae find out what you're good at, and as it turned out, I'm very good at crime. Jist a minute, please.'

He jumped up from his chair, slipped his glasses back on, and stepped over to Bruce's cage. Bruce had been chewing at the bars for a nut for several minutes, and Ronnie waited by the cage as he took ten sunflower seeds from his fingers. Bruce could pack 117 sunflower seeds into his cheeks at a time, that was the record, but Ronnie was busy just now. He returned to his chair, nodding wisely as the interviewer went on.

'Well,' Ronnie said, 'of course I'd be the last tae deny that a life of crime brings with it a certain – how can I put it – charismatic appeal, which has its advantages –'

He stopped, cut short. This interviewer was no idiot, and had found fame and respect because he understood the special qualities which had brought his guests to greatness. Deep down

Ronnie had no admiration for this sort of television, but he could play the game as well as anyone. He sounded more thoughtful as he fixed a sincere gaze on the area just above the sink.

'Yes I suppose it can be,' he said. 'Of course one always has friends and accomplices, but basically I've always been a loner, and that's the way I prefer tae operate.'

Across the road in the church hall, Mr Lucas the dance instructor peered through the leaded glass of a window. The boy in the ground-floor flat was showing off to someone in his room again. He was an odd-looking boy, with a flat face and glasses that looked as if they were stuck together with tape. As Mr Lucas watched, the boy jumped out of his seat, shouting. Mr Lucas sighed and went back to the piano.

Ronnie's face was purple with anger, and his finger shook as he held it in front of him, pointing threateningly at the draining board.

'What dae you mean?' he shouted. 'What dae you mean – unethical?'

There was a time when the joke shop had been the most important place in the world. Ronnie couldn't remember when he first went there, but he knew what it was he had bought – blood capsules. He had had a thing about blood capsules and fake injuries, and on evenings after school he and Fumble Jenkins used to go down the Gorgie Road and die in the middle of the pavement. Nobody ever paid any attention unless you collapsed on them, but it was something to do.

There were two main types of blood capsule, the wet and the dry. Wet ones were better for timing, because you only had to bite them and blood poured out. The dry ones had powder that you had to swill about your mouth and mix with saliva, but they did taste better. In the end he stuck mostly to the dry ones, because they were cheaper.

The blood capsules soon started to lose their glamour, and Ronnie homed in on the other things the joke shop had to offer. It had been there longer than anyone could remember, and it was just crammed with stuff. Baskets on the floor, cases and cupboards on the walls and hanging racks were littered with useful equipment.

He started with sugar. There was ordinary nasty sugar that just made tea taste horrible, then there was blue-dye sugar that turned it sort of black, and then there were sugar cubes with stuff in them. You could get almost anything inside a sugar cube. There were dried worms and plastic insects, wriggling bugs and even little rude things.

The shop was tucked away up a side street in Leith, about half an hour's walk from school, and wherever they moved him Ronnie always managed to get back there. As the years went by he got to know Mr Hardwick pretty well, and sometimes he would get a few pennies discount for being a regular customer.

Mr Hardwick had run the Joke and Novelty shop since the end of the war, and he was always sad. Sometimes he put on joke spectacles with boggling eyes that came out on springs and tried to be happy, but he was only pretending. 'There's no money in jokes anymore,' he said to Ronnie one day, and soon after that he put the advert in the paper for part-time help.

'You haven't got any qualifications,' he told Ronnie, but Ronnie described the sounds made by the four different sorts of bangers, showed how to stop a crazy golf ball moving for long enough to tee it up properly, and explained why Hong Kong plastic pimples were better than British ones at half the price.

Mr Hardwick said Ronnie had youth and enthusiasm and tried him out for six months at three afternoons a week. At first Ronnie used to jam his pockets with as much as he could possibly grab during an afternoon, until his locker was clogged with stacks of rubber insects and streamer sprays and slime. Then he and Will had a huge argument, and he ended up taking most of it back to the shop.

The fact was that by the time Mr Hardwick's wife's arthritis got really bad and he needed somebody to look after the shop for full days, Ronnie never wanted to see a joke again. He was embarrassed by what he'd done when he was less mature, and he was sick of selling the things to other people. He'd had it with jokes.

But there were four million people wanting a job, so Ronnie moved out of Care and became a Joke Shop Assistant. He also felt sorry for Mr Hardwick, and he knew he could manage the stock and the ordering better. Three months went by, and he sorted out the stock and ordering, got a £2-a-week rise, and moved from a hostel into the bedsit. Then he started thinking about his ambitions. He had lots.

It was very important to take a professional approach to achieving ambitions. The expedition to the Highlands with Will was a good example. It hadn't turned out exactly as planned, but it was good experience and another lesson learned. And it was important not to be discouraged. By the time Will appeared in the shop with the news that he'd given up his job, Ronnie was at an advanced stage of planning again.

The trouble with Will was that he was too moody. He lived in his own wee world, always had done. As Ronnie searched through the drawers for the secret weapon, Will just slumped across the counter, staring into space.

'I jist don't understand it,' he said.

Ronnie was doubly aggravated because he was sure he'd left the secret weapon in the snakes drawer, but it wasn't there. He scrabbled through the other drawers at the back of the counter, trying to keep Will's attention.

'Wait a minute, I've got it jist here, hang on,' he said.

Will hardly looked up. The secret weapon had fallen from the back of the snakes drawer, which was too full, into the false hands drawer. Ronnie held it up right in front of Will's nose so that Will could see it.

'D'ye know what this is?' Ronnie said.

Will shook his head. He looked almost apprehensive as Ronnie waved the secret weapon in front of him. Ronnie had made it himself, from a rubber ball and part of a plastic trumpet, and he was dead pleased with it. There probably wasn't another one like it anywhere in the world.

'This is the thing,' he said to Will. 'It's brilliant! They dinnae stand a chance now man.'

He waited excitedly for Will's reaction, and when nothing happened he hesitated, and then delved into another drawer for the mask. He slipped it over his head and reappeared above the counter.

'Whit dae you think?' he asked Will.

It was the best mask they had ever had in the shop. A clown de luxe, imported from America, and better than any clown Ronnie had seen. It had sticking-out teeth and a brilliant grin, wide eyes and real orange curly hair. Will looked as if he was just about to speak when the shop door opened and Mrs Paterson came in, blotting out the sunlight.

Ronnie had had trouble with Mrs Paterson before. She marched straight up to him, red-faced, plump, bull-necked, and stared him in the clown face. He could see the whites of her eyes.

'Have you been selling that nasty sugar to wee Angus again?' she bellowed.

The secret of successful lying is to believe that what you are saying is absolutely truthful. Ronnie tried hard to concentrate on this as he pulled off the clown mask, accidentally taking his glasses off with it. He squinted up at Mrs Paterson, whose face was only about six inches away.

'No,' he said, 'I . . .'

The first blow came from nowhere, fell full across the side of his head, and sent him reeling back against the wall. Then she was leaning over the counter, slapping and whacking him as he slid slowly down to his knees. She was the human steam-hammer, Attila the Hun Paterson, tamer of the saber-toothed tiger.

Ronnie slumped on the floor, his arms thrown vaguely across his head to try and protect it. He kept saying 'Aye . . . yes . . . right' as much as he could, for Mrs Paterson yelled as she hit.

'I've telt ye before WHACK Ronnie Wotherspoon WHACK if I catch you causing trouble WHACK WHACK with any o' ma bairns WHACK jist once more WHACK you'll have Mr Paterson down here, an' I'll no answer for the consequences. Ye stupid little bugger WHACK WHACK WHACK you're nothing WHACK but a waste WHACK o' good space.' WHACK WHACK.

And she stopped and turned away. Half way to the door she hesitated, and Ronnie started trying to climb inside the display case.

'An' I'll see that Mr Hardwick hears about this,' she shouted.

There was a long silence after the door slammed behind her. Ronnie stood up slowly, dusted his jeans, coughed, put on his glasses and looked at Will. He had glimpsed Will cringing in the corner, blinking as Mrs Paterson hit, and Will still looked very worried. They looked at each other.

Will said, 'I think I know where we can get a gun.'

- 4 -

Mother was in bed reading about deprived children. Mother loved deprived children, and had argued with Father about being foster-parents. Father said it was bad enough having two deprived children of their own.

Just after Christmas Mother had taken to cutting out pictures of little black children with sticking-out bellies from the papers, and then the letters started arriving from Africa, and she had to tell Father about Bobby. She had adopted him. Bobby was a little black boy, and every month Mother sent £5 to Africa and every three months a letter came back from the people in Africa saying that Bobby was very well. Father went spare.

Mother showed him the picture she had of Bobby and eventually Father shut up, though there was a hell of a fuss one Sunday when he found another picture in the family album. Bozl something was his real name. Will didn't mind coming from a multi-racial family, and Mother was quite excited because she said soon Bobby would be able to write to them, though none of them spoke any African. Ronnie said it was all a con and the money went to the white slave traders.

Lately Mother had been bringing home books on deprived children from the library and going to bed early, and Will wondered if the family was going to get any bigger. Father wouldn't like it.

Everything was very quiet. Father was in his armchair, reading the paper. Will sat on the settee, pulling threads out of the edge of the arm-cushion. Eventually he said, 'I've sort of stopped my job.' Father lowered his paper. 'Not fired, not got the sack, exactly, more sort of – resigned,' Will said quickly.

'Maybe sort of retired,' Isla said. She had appeared from nowhere, right in the doorway of the sitting-room. Father blew his stack at that. He whipped round in his seat, bellowing up the corridor where Isla had disappeared again, 'Isla, I'm telling you . . .'

The only sound that came back down the corridor was the flush of the toilet. Will knew Father wasn't really angry at Isla. Father had worked for the Gas Board for twenty-three years, man and boy, which made some things pretty hard for him to understand. Will braced himself.

Will left the house early next morning, saying that he was going to look for work. Things were going from bad to worse, and when he got to the joke shop it didn't take long to work out that Ronnie had had another idea.

A long time ago Ronnie had said he was going to be an inventor and make the perfect practical joke, until The Everlasting Banger set fire to the George Street newspaper-stand. Now here he was with a stupid-looking clown mask and a farting trumpet. He had invented it.

Ronnie had no idea how desperate things were. Strange, terrible thoughts were going through Will's mind. This was probably The Crossroads of Life, and here was Ronnie, trying on clown masks. Will wondered if it was his biorhythms.

Then Mrs Paterson came in and assaulted Ronnie. She hit him and hit him until he was all curled up behind the counter, and she kept hitting him. She had fists like bricks. Will didn't know what to do, and then he thought of the gun.

They took the bus to Wester Hailes and walked through the blocks of flats to the adventure playground. It was a nice afternoon, without many people around, and Will could see a young couple nestled together on a bench. He led Ronnie across the grass behind them, and tapped the girl on the shoulder.

'Whit the hell you doin'?' Isla shouted, jumping up from her seat. She was wearing her paramilitary gear, ammunition belt and holsters.

'Hi guys,' said Craigie Dixon, grinning up at them. Craigie was in the same class as Isla, and they had been going out for nearly a month now, though Isla had always said she didn't want to be tied down.

'Whit dae you two jokers want?' Isla shouted.

'Firepower,' said Ronnie.

Craigie had a lot of his stuff with him. His dad was in the territorial army, and Craigie had always had the best guns of any kid on the estate. He had a remote control boat that could go on the pond and fire little missiles, and Will had always wanted a shot of his machine-gun that fired real clay pellets from a cartridge belt. Craigie had twice been seen by the police for shooting over the fence at the rugby players in Myreside Park. The story on the estate was that he'd revolutionised the score in the Edinburgh Schools Rugby Cup Final that year.

Isla was tutting, and Will nudged Ronnie. 'Business,' Ronnie said, and jingled the coins in his jeans pocket.

Craigie brought out a sonic blaster from under the bench. It was big and white with a handle at the side that you turned, and he aimed it at two wifeys walking on the other side of the road. There was a piercing wailing noise from the gun, and the wifeys peered worriedly about them.

'Shhhh,' said Ronnie, waving for Craigie to put the gun down. 'Naw, I don't think that's quite it.'

Next Craigie brought out an old-fashioned ray gun, a real

beauty with yellow lightning stripes down the side of it. Will looked hopefully at Ronnie, but Ronnie was shaking his head already. Too advanced.

Isla rooted about under the bench, and brought out a small black gun. 'How about this?' she said.

It was a secret-agent gun, an automatic with simulated wooden handle. Ronnie took it and squinted along the sights, pointing at the sky, and then he stared inside the barrel, and then he tried the trigger. He looked as if he knew a lot about these things. Isla sighed loudly and started playing keepy-uppy with an invisible football. Will leant over beside Craigie and held out his left hand.

'Ever seen anythin' like this?' he said.

'Bugger me,' said Craigie, 'is that herpes?' He started counting. 'Can ye no' get them burnt off or somethin'?'

Will wasn't sure if it would be better to say it *was* herpes. Herpes was something you got on other bits of you, and those were all right the last time he looked. He was going to say something hopeful, but Craigie wasn't paying any attention anymore. Ronnie liked the gun.

'Fifty pee,' Ronnie said to Isla.

'Fifty pee? Dae you know how much somethin' like that costs in the shops?' Isla said.

'Aye that's right,' said Craigie. 'That's die-cast metal there, wi' a simulated wood handle. Ye canny get somethin' like that nowadays. But seein' as how I know ye, seventy-five.' He grinned importantly at Isla.

'Craigie Dixon you said I could have that gun, an' I'm no' partin' wi' it for under a pound,' Isla said.

Craigie shrugged. He'd been going out with Isla for nearly a month now, so he must have been a pacifist at heart.

Ronnie only had seventy-three pence in his pocket and Will had twenty-five and a half, so they got a bargain in the end. Craigie gave them a roll of caps, and Ronnie shook hands with him. Will held out his hand too, his good one, but Craigie just stared at it and shook his head.

On Tuesday they went into town to get the timetables. It was the height of the tourist season, but they'd spent their bus-fares on armaments, so there was no avoiding the walk. Will dodged along through the crowds behind Ronnie.

Ronnie had his own way of travelling. He put his head down and set his body squarely in the direction he wanted to go, and his legs went like the clappers. He never went so fast as when he was hammering through a crowd. Often people would stop and turn to shout, but nobody had reactions fast enough to grab him before he disappeared into the crush.

On Princes Street on a busy day it was the law of the jungle, he said. Will tried to get drawn along in Ronnie's slip-stream, but often he would find himself heading straight for a group of old people or a wifey with a pram or somebody trying to work out who had just battered past them, and he would have to abort. He ended up twirling and weaving like a boozy ballet dancer, raising his hands above his head to make himself as thin as possible, and apologising all the way.

So Will didn't get much of a chance to talk to Ronnie on the way to the tourist office. He caught up with him at Waverley Bridge, which had less people to the square foot, but then two back-packing Australians stopped him and asked him to take their photograph with the castle in the background.

At the tourist office Will and Ronnie stood in one of the long queues, watching Callum behind the desk at the front. Callum was trying to talk to an American woman who kept saying that even in Rome they managed to squeeze her in. Ronnie looked very grimly at Will and Will decided not to say anything.

He was sure that a fat woman in the next queue was staring at them. She was eating whole sticks of Edinburgh Rock from a tartan box, watching them. Behind them a father kept slapping a little boy who was screaming. On the other side of the room, a security man was arguing with a tourist who shouted and waved his arms. Will stood listening to Ronnie's teeth grinding until they reached the front of the queue.

'How ye doin', lads?' Callum said. 'Sorry about all this.'

Ronnie leaned over the counter, very businesslike, with his packet of cigarettes.

'Not bad, Callum, not bad. Want a fag?'

Callum had got off the dole to work in the tourist office for the summer. They had known him since Saughton Junior, but this was business. Will looked round. The security man was leading the shouting foreigner out of the office. The fat woman was still watching them, her mouth crammed full of rock.

'Oh, ye get used tae it,' Callum said. 'Naw, we're no' allowed tae smoke, but on ye go.'

Ronnie lit a cigarette and blew the smoke up at the ceiling. 'What d'ye have in the way of timetables for tourist buses, ye know, up North?' he said.

Callum started reaching in a drawer in his desk.

'Where is it ye're goin'?'

'Oh, could be anywhere, what have ye got?' Ronnie was being ultra-casual. He looked round meaningfully at Will. Will smiled politely. Callum was digging in drawers now, and the racks behind him, pulling out all sorts of leaflets and books.

'Well now, tours,' he said, 'there's Caledonian tours, that's simple, and the package agencies, now the Eastern Scottish ones, and the British Isles Tour Guide, I haven't got all the foreign ones, there's Scot-Tour and the Germans, and France-Écosse is catching on, oh and these, and wait, wait – yes these are probably the best ones.' He put three telephone-directory-size things on top of the great pile which had appeared on the desk, and smiled at Ronnie. 'Dutch, ye know,' he said.

Ronnie leaned over to Callum importantly. 'How much is all that?' he said.

'All of it? All together?' said Callum. He added up the total – many of them were free. It came to twenty-eight pounds. Ronnie stared at Callum.

'Aye, I know,' Callum said. 'Go on, take it, quick. And leave me a fag.'

Ronnie started grabbing a great bundle of leaflets, and Will scooped up a big armful. They weighed a ton, and he tried to tuck them under his chin. As they turned to go Ronnie fished in his jacket pocket with his free hand and threw a battered cigarette packet on the counter.

'You're a pal, Callum,' he said.

Aerobics had been inevitable in the Bryce home for months. Isla got her new satin-look leotard for Christmas, and she probably owned the biggest collection of exercise records in Edinburgh. Dance Yourself Fit with film stars, television personalities, even the Canadian Royal Air Force, she had them all. Then Mother took up classes once a week at the community centre, and she would practise while she was making the dinner. She could do knee-bends while she was grating carrots.

It was one of the few things that Will and Father agreed about. They hated it. Even the cat hated it; the first notes of any of Isla's records sent it whining for the door quicker than anything else. Father had nearly persuaded Mother it was aerobics that was making the cat pee all the time.

From the sitting-room Will could see Mother in the kitchen, jiggling about in the kitchen and rolling pastry to the music. Father was sitting at the table, complaining. Isla was right by the stereo, bending in two and doing the splits like Rubberwoman, and speaking along with the record. She knew them all by heart.

'Neck bend, turn your head, shake your body, shake your body.'

Will tried to watch her, not Ronnie. Ronnie had taken his jacket off, and his breathing was getting hoarser. The floor shook every time he landed. Will could hear Father saying, 'For God's sake'. The music was very loud. He watched Mother kiss Father on the head as she passed with the pastry dish. Mother said, 'It's like the old days, like we're a family again.'

Suddenly Ronnie stopped jumping. He looked at his watch and shouted at Will between horrible gasps. 'We've got nine hours and forty-seven minutes tae go,' he panted. 'Whit's wrong wi' you?'

Will didn't like it, but he'd watched Isla enough to know what

28

you were supposed to do. 'Ye're no' doin' it right,' he said. 'Ye need tae try an' loosen your neck more.'

Ronnie's face was going red as he shouted, and his veins and tendons were sticking out. 'We're a team, right?' Ronnie yelled over the music. 'Whit's the point o' half the bloody team being in training?'

Then Ronnie moved in even closer to Isla and jumped and clomped like he was trying to beat the carpet. Isla danced about, bent down, put her elbows on the ground, looked back between her legs and saw Ronnie, and that was that. She was furious.

'Are you trying tae be funny?' she screamed at Ronnie. 'I'll put your face back, ye big idiot,' and she stormed out of the room.

Ronnie went straight for the stereo, threw off the disco music, and slapped on a single. It was the theme music to one of the *Rocky* films. Music for heroes. Ronnie was away again, shadow-boxing round the room and making strange surf-like noises, but also talking, after a fashion. 'Excitement . . . confidence . . . power . . . tae be champions . . . build oursels' tae be the tops . . . the kings . . . the killers . . . number one.'

Will understood. He had talked to Ronnie, and Ronnie had it all worked out, although Will didn't like to think about it too much. Thinking and warts were pretty low priority now. The music battered away, and Will was standing on the settee, gently bouncing up and down on the springs, his eyes shut, his arms raised above his head. The Kings . . . The Killers . . . Number One. Only very distantly did he hear Isla's voice drifting through from the kitchen.

'Eighteen years old . . . you'd never believe it.'

Before Ronnie went home they stood on the balcony, looking out over the twinkling lights of the city. The floodlit castle floated above the street lights far away. The sky was clear, and, without a moon, the stars seemed brighter than usual.

'Nice night,' Ronnie said.

Will felt terrible. He tried to answer, but a coughing grunt was all that came out.

Ronnie quietly said, 'How do you feel?'

Will made a great effort to pull his thoughts together. It took him a long time. He sighed. 'Mum says the thing for a wart is gold. Ye rub it with a gold ring or something and it goes away. Do ye think?'

'Aye,' Ronnie said, 'well, yes, she could be right ye know, aye, I have heard that.'

There was a pause. 'Oh good,' Will said.

– 5 –

The bus rolled through the winding mountain roads, sunlight flashing through the forest shadows in its single row of big windows. Inside, its sixty-eight passengers were busy with the first chatter of the morning's travel.

Esme Proctor watched them sourly from her swivelling seat at the front of the coach. They were a typical bunch for that tour; mostly middle-aged or elderly, mostly couples, a lot of Americans wearing bits of tartan, the odd German and French couple, a few Dutch people. One vegetarian meals, one travel-sickness pills, two who needed a hand getting on and off. Nothing she couldn't handle.

Esme rubbed her eyes discreetly. She'd got plastered at the hotel bar with Harry the driver while the tourists were in the ballroom the night before, and she was beyond the healing powers of a Traditional Scottish Breakfast. Harry winked sympathetically at her.

He'd had more practice at this sort of thing – he'd been doing the Bonnie Prince Charlie tour for years. It was a two-nighter, travelling northwards into the more remote Highlands on a circuit from Edinburgh. Esme groaned under her breath and wished she'd stayed on day excursions.

Up the aisle Mrs Bechstein was still going on about her clan tartan – 'plaid', she called it – and Esme could hear some foreign babble with the words 'Loch Ness' cropping up all the time, though the bus was going nowhere near the Loch. Away at the back Mr Bender leaned his head slowly into her line of vision and winked. Esme sighed and swivelled round to face the front. He was a bottom-slapper.

Harry put on his sunglasses. There was a fine clear sky, and the cameras started snapping as the coach sped up the green mountain passes towards Glen Lochart. The second day of the BPC tour was always the bleakest. It followed the deserted northern roads, with not a village, a car or another human being for miles. It was wild, beautiful country, but the sun was much too bright for Esme's tender eyes.

Reluctantly she picked up the microphone and switched it on. She smiled a cheery smile up the coach, wincing quietly at the facial strain, and pointed her head at the window.

'And now on your right you can see some of the most spectacular scenery in Scotland,' she said. 'The mountain rising in the centre of the range is Ben Lochart, and in a cave on the far side, Bonnie Prince Charlie is said to have taken refuge from the Redcoats.'

Esme glanced back up the aisle. Marvellous. They were all staring in exactly the wrong direction, out of the left-hand window. This always happened. Wearily she pointed her head leftwards and continued.

'And to the left . . .' She hesitated. There was something moving in her field of vision. She strained to focus her eyes. A motorbike, riding parallel to the coach, on the grass. It was coming closer, faster, overtaking. And on the motorbike there was a clown – a clown, like a circus clown, with red hair and a little black hat on the top. And sitting behind the clown was a wolfman in a green jacket with a rucksack on its back. And the wolfman was waving at her.

Esme looked up the bus. The passengers were all leaning up at the windows, and some of them were waving back to the wolfman. Esme lifted her arm and waved too, slowly. The motorbike came on to the road in front of the bus and started to slow down, and the wolfman waved for Harry to stop.

'Esme . . . Esme – what is it?' Harry was shouting at her. He slowed the bus to a stop.

'Motorbike,' Esme said.

It was parked in front of the bus now, but the clown and the wolfman had disappeared. Esme looked up the road. It was deserted. Suddenly there was a banging, and Esme swivelled round. They were at the door, the clown with the red hair and the wolfman with the rucksack, banging on it. Harry opened the door, and up the steps they came.

The clown was first. Very gently it put its hand down to Esme's lap. She looked down. It was taking the microphone out of her hand. It lifted it up and turned to face the passengers, with the wolfman standing behind, beside Esme.

The clown spoke into the microphone. 'This is a hold –' it said, but the wolfman interrupted, waving something in the air.

'This is a gun,' the wolfman shouted. Esme felt a strange floating sensation. It was quite nice. The wolfman had a gun. The clown started talking into the microphone again, impatiently. 'Please put all your money and jewellery in the bag here,' it said.

The wolfman squeezed past and started to move up the aisle, carrying its haversack, and waving the gun. A tall, skinny wolfman. The clown stayed at the front of the bus, watching. Esme swivelled her seat to see what was happening. Harry was leaning his head on the steering wheel, having a rest. Esme peered round the stocky body of the clown.

The passengers were all very quiet, watching the wolfman with the gun. This was a surprise for them. They were putting things into the wolfman's haversack. Money, she could see them putting in wads of notes, and some of the ladies were taking off rings and necklaces and – there, that was Mrs Bechstein's real pearl necklace that just went into the haversack.

Suddenly the clown gave a little jump, as if it had forgotten something. 'And watches!' it shouted. Esme could see passengers unbuckling their watches. They were very serious, concentrating on putting things into the bag.

Somebody was standing up at the back of the coach. It was Mr

Bender. Oh dear, Esme thought, he'd better not try to slap her bottom while this was going on.

Mr Bender came up the aisle towards her. He was wearing his Hawaiian pattern shirt – he had the worst shirts Esme had ever seen. He walked very slowly, holding his hands up at waist level in front of him, and staring at the wolfman. The wolfman stopped moving, and stood very still. It had probably caught sight of Mr Bender's shirt.

'Okay sonny,' Mr Bender said, 'just back off gently and no-body's going to get hurt.' He sounded very relaxed. He was getting closer and closer to the wolfman, until he was nearly touching it.

'Give me the gun,' he said reaching out for it. The wolfman still didn't move.

With a shout the clown jumped up the aisle behind the wolfman and pulled something out of a pocket. It was round, with a brightly coloured trumpet-like spout. The clown pointed it over the wolfman's shoulder, and suddenly there was a big white cloud round Mr Bender's head. Esme grinned. This was the best bit.

Then the clown and the wolfman were running back up the aisle towards her. They stopped for a moment at the door, looking at each other, and the wolfman jumped off with the haversack. The clown looked at Esme and looked at Harry, and then held out its hand to Harry. Harry shook it, looking up at the clown. Then the clown held out a hand to Esme. It wore woolly gloves. Esme shook the hand, smiling. Never ever, when she had gone to the circus, had the clown come up and shaken her hand.

'Pleased to meet you,' the clown said.

Then it jumped out of the door and ran to the motorbike. Esme watched as it got on in front of the wolfman and started the engine. She watched as the bike disappeared up the road, with the wolfman waving its arms, and the motorbike weaving about happily from side to side of the road. She was sure she could hear them shouting and whooping.

When Esme looked back up the bus, Mr Bender was lying on the floor. The top part of his body was covered in a kind of white powder, and he was groaning and coughing and scratching at his horrible shirt. Every so often he bunched up and gave a great loud sneeze. He didn't look well.

The passengers sitting in the seats nearby were shrinking back, staring at him as he squirmed and spluttered. The powder was all over the carpet. Esme's head ached again as she looked for a cloth to clear up the mess.

Ronnie lay full-length on top of the joke-shop counter, his favourite place, trying to blow smoke-rings. The future was coming along nicely.

He quite often visited the shop in the evenings since Mr Hardwick gave him the key. He didn't like to leave Bruce for too long, but sometimes he had to stay in the shop late to do the accounts, and sometimes he just stayed anyway. There was something satisfying about sitting in the darkened shop after closing, surrounded by boxes of fart gas and black-face soap, watching people drift by in the street outside. It made him feel official.

'Steaks,' he said, holding up his thumb and forefinger two inches apart.

'Steaks that thick, wi' mashed tatties – *creamed* tatties, and peas, and – onion rings. And chocolate milk shakes. And brandy. Every day. Three times.'

He had never been that concerned about food. He didn't mind living on jam sandwiches for a year when he was saving up for the bike, and if it came to a choice between eating and doing something important, his stomach could take care of itself. But he knew about good food. He knew from the sorts of things people bought him if they took him from the home for a trial meal when he was younger. Now he could afford it, Ronnie was going to dine like a king.

The shop was lit up for a minute by a car turning outside. Ronnie inhaled a mouthful of smoke and tapped at his cheek, sending a stream of tiny smoke-rings upwards in the light.

'My bum hurts,' Will said, shifting on the ground. 'It's dead bumpy, ye know.'

Will had a lot to learn, but he was all right. He got scared of the masks hanging on the walls when it was dark, but he didn't seem to mind just now. He sat on the floor, leaning his back against the counter, staring into space as usual.

People like Ronnie always had a faithful sidekick. Ronnie grinned down at his faithful sidekick.

'Ye get used tae it. No, she's runnin' like a dream, firin' jist right, an' we need shock absorbers like that for whit we want tae dae.'

It was true. The bike was a Roadburner 125, not the biggest bike in the world, but a superb machine. They didn't make them any more, of course, but Ronnie's would last a lifetime. It had wing mirrors and a tachometer and indicators – the works. It had taken Ronnie nearly a year and a half to buy it, but it had been worth it.

'What was in that bloody puffer thing?' Will said, craning round. 'It was brilliant.'

Ronnie spat on his cigarette butt to put it out and flicked it on the floor.

'Itching powder, sneezing powder, curry powder, sting powder, vim, pepper, athlete's foot powder,' he said. 'And some stuff I got out of an old firework.'

'It was brilliant. How did ye know it would work?'

'I tested it on Ally Mathewson's wee brother.'

Ally Mathewson's wee brother had put a very horrible thing on the seat of Ronnie's bike when it was parked outside the shop the week before, so it was fair enough that he should help Ronnie with the experiment. Ronnie had only used a very small sample of the powder. He wondered about the man on the bus. It was very unlikely it would be fatal.

Will looked happy. 'That little brandy worked great as well,' he said.

The brandy had been Ronnie's idea too. He had thought of it last year when he did his motorbike test. He passed first time. A miniature bottle was just the right dose, if you drank it down in one gulp.

'Five star,' Ronnie said. 'Two days' wages. I'll nip down the Paki tomorrow and get a crate.'

A noisy crowd of folk went by the door of the shop, on their way to the disco. Ronnie lit another cigarette and tried blowing smoke-rings again.

Will sighed. He was looking very closely at his left hand, trying to get it in the light that came through the door from the street lamp outside.

'No,' Will said, looking at his hand, 'but it's terrible now, ye know, we cannae dae anything.' Ronnie sat up.

'Well if we start spending all this money, they're goin' tae notice, aren't they?' Will said. 'Everybody knows we dinnae have any money.'

Ronnie didn't know what had got into Will. He was so unpredictable, and it was becoming tiresome.

Will turned to face him, looking worried. 'We'll have tae get good jobs wi' good wages before we can spend any o' this,' he said.

That was ridiculous. Will had no idea. If it hadn't been for Ronnie, Will would never even have done it in the first place. And now he was getting the whole thing tangled up in technicalities, as if it wasn't a success at all, and the plan had gone wrong somewhere. What did he expect them to do?

'An' whit about ma steaks?' Ronnie said.

Will looked round the room as if he was searching for an idea hanging on the wall.

'Maybe we could have a fund,' he said. 'Like a pension fund, like fer footballers when they get past it. Then we could dae somethin' really special.' He looked up hopefully.

Well at least he was trying. 'Aye, somethin' really special,' Ronnie said. 'Yes, well, maybe, I'd been thinkin' of somethin' along those lines.'

Ronnie grinned and slapped his hands on the counter. 'Anyway, pal, it's not the money that counts anymore now. You and me, we're bigger than, well – ' he thought – 'something very very big. We've made it. We're in the big time. The big time.'

Will was looking at his hand again.

'I'm not holding up any trains,' he said.

Ronnie spread everything out on the bedsit floor to take stock. In the spotlight of the anglepoise lamp he counted the money – £544 in all. Most of it was in tens and twenties, but Will had been collecting coins as well. There was £18 in coppers.

The jewellery was in all shapes and sizes. There were a number of rings, lots of bracelets in copper and silver and wood, a string of pearls, fancy earrings, and seventeen watches, but no really classy ones. Ronnie didn't know what to do with them once they were spread all over the floor, so he made a nut trail around them for Bruce. Bruce wasn't interested.

Bear was. She sat against the wall, squinting at all the jewellery with her one eye. Bear was very old and battered but she wasn't a teddy bear. She was just a sort of souvenir. Ronnie had done operations on her when he was younger, and he knew her inside-out.

Ronnie put on his Arab accent to speak to Bear, dribbling the pile of rings through his fingers.

'You like, huh? You want?' he said. Bear squinted back, and Ronnie pulled her into the light under the lamp.

'See,' he said, twirling a necklace, 'Egyptian gold, beaten by hand and polished with the blood of native craftsmen.'

He dropped the necklace and picked up a string of pearls, which he draped over Bear's neck. It suited her.

'You are a proud woman, but I can give you more than you have ever dreamed of possessing,' he said, staring into her eye. He was fitting bangles, rings, even a glow-in-the-dark digital watch on to her. Bear looked as pleased as punch. She gazed back at Ronnie, tenderly.

'All this can be yours!' he said, picking up a pile of tenners and throwing them into the air so that they fell like confetti over Bear's head. Then he leant down so that his nose was right by hers. 'If you will be my wife.'

Will hardly slept at all that night. Father and Mother had gone to bed when he came in, and he felt okay until he slumped into his own bed. He was tired, it had been a busy day, but suddenly it crept up on him – it wasn't really right.

Was it? Ronnie had a point, there were a million things that weren't right, but a million and one wrongs don't make a right. Was that right? Will kept slipping into sleep, and he would see a fat man in a horrible shirt come grinning up an alley towards him, carrying a hangman's noose; or Father and Mother sitting opposite him in court, blubbering; or worst of all, Isla and her friends grilling him with sonic blasters. Then he would wake up and try to work it out again.

When they had done it, when they jumped off the bus and on the bike and raced away through the hills, it was brilliant. It couldn't be right. It couldn't. He thought of writing to Mary-Jane Allen in the problem page at the back of the TV Guide, but they probably had experts that could trace him to Wester Hailes by his handwriting or the ink he used.

Will could hear Mother in the kitchen and Father shouting to Isla to get out of the bathroom. The worst thing was, he'd have to sit there, in front of them, knowing what he'd done. He sat up and pulled on a sweater and jeans, and looked out of the window. It was cloudy. He could see three kitchens lit up in the opposite block, and people moving about. Will often stared across at the other blocks, wondering about the people inside, but he never saw anything rude.

The front door slammed as Isla left for school. He got up and shuffled through to the kitchen.

Father was sitting at the kitchen table, reading the paper. He spoke to Will without looking up. 'Good morning, son.' He never said that if Will got up at the proper time. Mother was washing the dishes. She smiled at him.

'Morning,' Will said, sitting down. Father still didn't look up. He was in a sarcastic mood.

'I take it,' Father said, 'we are tae believe your ceaseless quest for an honest day's work has been in vain once more.' Then he looked at Will. He got these words from doing the crossword in the paper every day.

Will didn't know what to say. He looked at the fake woven-straw place-mat in front of him. He felt like apologising, but all he said was 'Uhuh'. There was a smear of dark-red tomato sauce hardened in one of the plastic loops of the mat.

Father stopped being sarcastic and leant forward. 'Well I'll tell ye what son, ye did bring it on yoursel'.' He sounded quite sorry for Will.

Mother put a plate of eggs and bacon in front of him and started clearing the table. He prodded at the egg yolks with a fork.

Mother said, 'How's Ronnie getting on with his job at the shop?'

Will stopped prodding. What did she want to ask about Ronnie for? 'Fine,' he said.

'He's enjoying it, is he?' Mother said.

'Aye,' said Will.

'Poor Ronnie,' said Mother. One time, years ago, when Will was alone with her in the kitchen she got serious and quiet and said, 'Will, what would you think of having Ronnie as a brother?' He knew what Father would have said to something like that.

'Ha!' Father said suddenly, slapping his paper with his open hand. Will jumped. Father read out loud from the paper, 'Police are today searching for two young Scots who held up and robbed a coachload of tourists on a remote Highland road.' He looked up at Will. 'What d'ye think of that then?'

Will's insides felt very weird. He stared across the table at Father, but Father was smiling. Did he know, all along? Were the police waiting in the hall, even now, to come in after Father explained how he had tracked Will down and how Will broke down and confessed? Will's stomach rumbled louder than he'd ever heard it before. Father gave him a weary look, and read on from the paper.

'The youths, dressed in theatrical disguises, followed the busy coach on a motorbike and forced it to stop at gunpoint.' He snorted happily. 'They took an estimated six hundred pounds in cash and an unknown quantity of valuables from the seventy frightened passengers before riding off at high speed into the hills again.'

Father slapped the newspaper down against his knee and sat back in his chair. He looked as if somebody had just given him a pools cheque. 'Now that is bloody clever,' Father said. 'I mean, who would have seen?' He leaned over the table, pointing gleefully at Will. 'Now there's enterprise for ye,' he said. 'Ha!' Then he was reading again. 'Foreigners, largely from Germany and the United States . . .'

Father liked it. He had misunderstood the whole thing, he didn't know anything about it, and he liked it. Will gripped the edges of his seat, conscious of his warts against the plastic. He opened his mouth, and out came 'But . . .' Father looked up suspiciously. Will squeezed the seat-edge harder. 'But don't ye think that's sort of really a bad thing tae do – rob people that – never did ye any harm?'

Mother was patting Will on the shoulder. 'Och yes of course it is, Will, don't you listen to your father, he's nothing but an old crook anyway,' she said.

Father put the paper down on the table in front of him. He looked seriously at Mother, and then at Will. Then he took off his glasses.

'Listen,' Father said, 'the Gas Board isnae exactly the Little Sisters of the Poor, but look at this –' he pointed at the newspaper in front of him – 'a couple o' young lads that have the wit and style tae take six hundred quid off a bunch of bloody tourists – and God knows they probably spend that much on plastic bagpipes in an afternoon at Boat of Garten – well these lads can have my vote any day o' the week.'

Will stared at Father. It was the longest thing he had ever heard him say. Will loved him. Father was putting on his glasses again, and picked up the paper. He read, 'Mrs Barbara Ginsberg of Winville, Vermont said, "This has never happened to me before!"'

Father burst out laughing, his mouth open and his head rocking on his neck. Will started to laugh too. It built up inside him as he watched Father, and suddenly he just doubled up with mirth, and he couldn't stop.

They waited a week before they did the second bus. Ronnie was worried about over-exposure, and he wanted to plan the route carefully. It was going to be a day-excursion coach on a trip from Edinburgh, so they wouldn't have so far to travel, but they'd have to be careful, he said.

Will was excited. He kept going into the joke shop to try on the wolfman mask in the back room, and he even borrowed a comb of Isla's to keep its hair in trim, until Isla found out he'd taken it. He told her he wanted to be smart for job interviews.

Ronnie was happier than Will had ever seen him, and it was difficult to persuade him not to give up the job at the joke shop straight away. Ronnie bought all the papers that had stories about them, and started keeping a file. He loved watching it on the telly as well, and every day he went down to the post office to see if they had wanted posters of them. Will liked seeing things about the wolfman in the paper too, but he felt as if the wolfman was somebody else, not really him. Ronnie knew it was Ronnie Wotherspoon the fuss was about.

They left Edinburgh at mid-morning, scheduled to meet the coach on an empty stretch of Perthshire road just before noon. Ronnie had bought a brand new map, and they clattered quickly through back-road villages and forests in the morning sun. Will's helmet rattled about on his head since the lining had gone, but the smell had gone with it, and when they were among the mountains he was able to swap it for his mask. They parked the bike in the middle of the road on a wide bend, and sat waiting for the bus to come round the corner.

Listening to the grinding of Ronnie's teeth, Will realised he could hear the sound of his own stomach rumbling as well. It was probably like actors going on stage: no matter how many times they did it, they still got nervous. When you were really nervous, all sorts of things happened to you. Maybe the cat's problem was just nerves, living in the same house as Isla.

Gradually the grindings and rumblings were joined by the sound of gears changing as the coach chugged through the twists of the forest road. Ronnie held up one hand in front of him and as the coach came round the corner he aimed his gun with the other. For a moment Will thought it wasn't going to stop. It came closer and closer till it was almost touching the bike. They heard a hiss as the door opened.

Ronnie was first up, and he took the microphone from the courier. She was a very pretty girl, sitting on the special seat at the front, and as Will stared at her she stared straight back, smiling a little.

'Hullo,' Ronnie said into the microphone. 'You might have heard of us, we were in the papers last week.'

The passengers were all craning to see what was happening at the front of the bus, but none of them said anything. Ronnie shifted about on his feet, waving the gun in the air. 'This is our gun,' he said.

'Gun,' said Will pointing to the waving gun: it was important. He glanced back at the courier. She was still staring at him, and still smiling. She had short curly brown hair and brown eyes. He tried to concentrate on the business.

Ronnie said, 'My pal the wolfman will now come down among you and collect your cash, jewellery – and watches.'

As he started off down the aisle, Will gave a small bow. He hoped she had noticed. He was going to be a model robber this time, and as the Americans fished out their valuables and dropped them in his bag his manners were perfect. They had no reason to look so upset.

'Super,' he said, 'wonderful . . . great, magic . . . thanks a lot.' Some old wifey tried giving him wooden bangles, but he gently pushed her hand away. 'You just hang on to that, dear,' he said kindly. A woman with blue hair gave him a necklace with rubies in it, and he held it up to catch the light, saying politely, 'Well isn't that bonny.' He was even taking the stuff stylishly, making a big flourish with his arm when he had to stretch to take a handful of jewellery or a wad of notes. And when he glanced up the bus the courier was still watching him, smiling round from behind Ronnie. This was the life.

Somebody was humming *Waltzing Matilda* loudly, and Will did a little jig now as he moved up the aisle. His pre-show nerves had gone completely, and he was enjoying himself. An old woman with glasses held up a twenty and said, 'I've got to have ten pounds to get back to the airport.'

Will started fishing in his bag, sorting through the notes. He thought he had a five, but there wasn't enough change. 'Has anyone got a five pound note?' he shouted up the bus. A man three rows back stood up, although his wife seemed to be trying to stop him, and said 'I've got five singles.' Will took the money, added his own fiver, and gave them to the woman with glasses, taking her twenty. 'Thank you, young man,' she said. Will looked happily up the aisle. The courier was laughing now.

It was getting noisy, and something had happened to the passengers. They were talking among themselves, and one angry man stood up and shouted, 'So who do we make the cheques out to?' Will was about to explain that they couldn't take cheques, but then a girl stood up as well, and said, 'This can't be serious.'

'Right then, pal.' It was Ronnie's voice, deadly serious, coming through the bus loudspeakers. Will grabbed a charm bracelet and a wallet that were still held out to him, and hurried back up the aisle. A lot of people were shouting things at him. As he got to the front, Ronnie yelled a quick 'See you' into the microphone, and jumped off the bus.

Will looked at the courier. She was watching him, with that little smile. She had such a pretty face. She said, 'You're a long way from Transylvania.' Will nodded. He had no idea what she meant. Distantly he could hear Ronnie revving the bike, and out of the corner of his eye he could see people coming up the aisle towards him. She glanced up at the noise, and suddenly he turned and jumped down the steps. He ran to the bike without looking back, and Ronnie took off at top speed.

By the time they got to the riverbank, Ronnie was fuming. He had stopped talking, and was just making grunting and groaning noises as he manoeuvred the bike through the trees. He cut the engine and got off, lighting a cigarette through the mouth of the clown mask. Then he stamped about, swearing. Still sitting on the bike, Will watched as Ronnie went to a clump of wild flowers at the edge of the clearing and pulled out the crash helmets and the number plates. He watched as Ronnie stopped, put them down, and came back over to him.

'Absolutely not,' Ronnie said. 'No.'

Will pulled off his mask and stared at Ronnie. He didn't know what to say, he just knew what was going to happen.

'It's not on,' Ronnie said, getting businesslike. 'It's not on, really. Come on, let's get the plates changed and get out of here.'

He bent down at the back of the bike and started unscrewing the plate. Will stared at him until he looked up again. Their eyes met, and Ronnie stood up, grunting.

'Have you gone soft in the heid or somethin'?' Ronnie shouted.

Will looked away. He was sorry. Ronnie threw his screwdriver into the grass as hard as he could.

'Shit!' he said.

Margot had heard about the coach-robbers, of course. It was the talk of the bus station, even though the robbery had been on another bus from another company. Some people were getting worked up about it, some thought it was all a great practical joke, and most of the couriers were quite intrigued. Everybody joked that they were going to be the next to be held up.

Then she came round a corner in the Perthshire Tour bus and the highwaymen were sitting in the middle of the road in front of the speeding coach. They didn't even have a proper motorbike, it was a little Japanese moped thing, with pedals in case the kick-start didn't work. And they themselves looked so odd – the clown was short and stocky, and the wolfman was long and skinny, and their masks were terrific. As soon as she saw them, she loved them.

You couldn't see much of their real faces, just the eyes. The clown had small, intense eyes, that flitted about over everything. And the wolfman, he had big gentle blue eyes. Neither of them could have been over twenty.

It wasn't like a real robbery at all. The clown told the passengers what to do on the microphone, and then the wolfman went collecting with his bag. But the clown looked embarrassed, just watching, and he started humming *Waltzing Matilda* to himself. And he'd forgotten he was holding the microphone, so his humming went right through the bus, and the wolfman was dancing away to it.

The passengers had a job taking it seriously, and Margot thought the robbers were going to get grabbed. She tried to talk to the wolfman, but he didn't answer.

It took a while to calm the passengers down, though nobody was very upset. You don't carry your dearest possessions or great amounts of money to go for a bus ride in the country. The wealthy ones were insured up to the eyeballs anyway. Apart from the usual girners, most of them seemed dazed by the whole thing.

The bus had been travelling for twenty minutes or so when the passengers started fussing again. It was something coming up the verge on the left side of the bus. Margot pressed up against the glass door, and she could see it was the motorbike. A few of the men were banging angrily on the windows, but as the bike came up the side of the bus they sat back quietly in their seats. The wolfman was waving his gun at them.

The bike drew level with the door, and the wolfman was carrying something else, and waving at her. It was a bunch of flowers, he was holding a bunch of wild flowers. He stretched it up towards her, and she struggled to open the window. The bus must have been going at fifty miles an hour. She leaned her arm out as far as it could go, and took the flowers.

By the time she had pulled them in, the bike had braked sharply and was turning behind the bus. She stuck her head out of the window and blew a kiss after it. Then she shut the window and turned to the back of the bus to watch the robbers disappearing in the opposite direction.

The wolfman turned and waved, and Margot waved back. Several of the passengers were scowling at her, but she could see one or two looking out of the back window too, waving at the bike as it vanished from sight. The smell of wild flowers drifted through the bus as she sat back in her seat.

− 7 −

It often rained in the cemetery. Generally that was a good thing, because it kept people away. It was full up, so it wasn't a busy place anyway.

Ronnie sat huddled beside the two gravestones. The wet grass was seeping through to his bum, and he knew it would feel worse when he got up. He lit a cigarette. This was the first time he'd been since things had started happening. He took a deep breath.

'There's no much tae tell this week,' he said. Raindrops were falling on his cigarette.

'Mr Hardwick wants me tae stay on at the shop still, but I don't know.' The cigarette went out. He scrabbled in his pocket for the matches, and the first three he pulled out of the box were spent. 'Bangers have been going very well,' he said. Will was always trying to get him to be tidy with used matches. It took him two goes to get lit again.

'Mrs Paterson sort of beat me up again. Didnae hurt very much.'

He threw all the spent matches on to the ground. Nobody bothered to cut the grass here now. He blew a half-hearted smoke-ring.

'I'm still on thirty a day.' It was more like forty, but he could cut down any time. In fact, he could stop altogether if he really wanted to, just like that. The rain tapped quietly at the stones, and Ronnie cleared his throat and spat.

'I saw Gail Atkinson on Monday, she's left Davy again, she said he hit her. I still don't like her though. Bruce has been getting really fat, god ye should see him, he just wobbles about eating and shitting the whole time, hardly ever goes on his exercise wheel. I think I'm giving him too much nuts. The weather's been good, apart from today.'

Ronnie hesitated for a minute. He looked around the cemetery and back at the two headstones. 'Did ye know that?'

He flicked a dod of ash on to the grass. It was funny how someone like him could get into a bad spell as far as communicating was concerned. He looked down at his shoes, which had bits of wet grass stuck to them.

'I've been holdin' up buses. I mean robbin' them, me an' Will Bryce, taking all the tourists' pocket money.'

There was nothing to be ashamed about in taking your life into your own hands and making something of yourself. It was called success. Ronnie smiled. 'We've been on the telly an' everything,' he said. 'I'm really quite enjoying it.'

He tamped the cigarette butt into the wet grass. 'I'll try not to get into trouble. Anyway,' Ronnie stood up and wiped down his trousers, 'I've got to get back.'

He hesitated for a minute, watching the two gravestones. Then he gave them a quick nod and started walking up the hill to the main road. His bum was soaked through.

Business was slow in the joke shop. Ronnie had a suspicion it was something to do with the new place in the centre of town, the Fun Den. It was all flashing neon signs and electronic gadgets and 'theatrical costumes', and it was always crowded with kids. At the Fun Den they charged fifteen pence for a single blue-mouth sweet, and people bought them. Ronnie knew you could get a box of a hundred straight from Taiwan for that much.

But it didn't bother him in the slightest. Blue-mouth sweets weren't his life anymore. He leaned on the counter with the

47

Standard cutting beside him – 'Perthshire Pirates' Daring Raid' – running through the latest collection in his mind.

'Eighty pounds,' he said, dribbling a lump of green slime between his fingers.

Will said, 'No' too long and no' too wide, and no' turny-down at the bottom. And no' piggish. A perfect nose.'

Ronnie hardly heard him. Will was off in his dream world. 'Eighty pounds he had in his wallet,' Ronnie said. 'Just pulled it out an' dropped it in the bag.' He looked at Will. 'Eighty pounds ye know!'

Will looked up. 'Aye, I know,' he said. 'It was me he gave it to.'

'How much was it?'

'Eighty pounds.'

There was someone at the door. Ronnie grabbed the newspaper cutting and threw it on the floor at his feet, and flung the ball of slime into a coffee cup, quickly trying to scrape worms of slime off his fingers on the rim. A policeman was coming into the shop.

The policeman walked over to the row of cabinets on the left, peering carefully into them. Ronnie glanced at Will. Will was gaping at him, his mouth opening and closing. His stomach was making a noise like a drain.

The policeman was studying the baskets on the floor now, the dog jobbies and chewing-gum wrapped contraceptives and the strap-on noses. Then he moved over to the racks. He still hadn't looked up at the counter.

Ronnie thought very very fast. It was a question of whether they had men at the back door. He could get through and out of it and over the wall into Mrs Grossart's garden before the policeman crossed the counter, and then he could sprint along the garden walls to Duke Street, up Market Lane and catch a number 29 out to Oxgangs. He had the fare in his pocket. But what about Will?

The policeman was coming over to the counter. Ronnie smiled at him, and the policeman looked warily at Will and leaned over the counter.

'Dae ye have any false tits?' he said.

Ronnie stared at the policeman.

48

'Medium or large?' he said.

The policeman's cheeks had gone quite red. 'How much are they?'

'Medium, four pounds seventy-five, large, six pounds fifty.' Ronnie was answering automatically. It took a while to adjust.

'Medium, please,' the policeman said.

Ronnie pulled the tits out of the drawer and placed them on the counter, took a fiver from the policeman and gave him the change and receipt. There was silence. The policeman was still standing there.

'Do you think you could put it in a bag or something?' he said eventually.

After he had gone, Ronnie and Will didn't say anything for a long time. Ronnie was ashamed that he'd let such thoughts into his head when the policeman had come in the door. As if anyone could even suspect their true identities. He busied himself with collecting the green slime out of the coffee cup, and trying to wipe the coffee off it with his hanky.

Will said, 'We have to find her.'

Ronnie stopped what he was doing. 'Who?'

Will was determined. He was staring at Ronnie. 'You know. Her.'

Then the door opened, and Wee Angus walked in. Ronnie jumped round the counter and ran towards him, grabbing him by the shoulders and dragging him back towards the door, pushing and slapping him. Wee Angus looked amazed. Ronnie hustled him right out on to the step, shouting all the way.

'No, no way, never again, get out, out, right out now! Okay!' He slammed the door.

After closing, they tramped along St Stephen Street towards the bedsit in the fading daylight. It was important that Will came to terms with the reality of their situation. It was a question of professionalism. On the last trip Will had been less than professional on a number of counts. He had endangered the success of the mission by being immature on the bus, and then he had insisted on going back to the same bus to be immature again.

49

'How do ye think ye could find her?' Ronnie said, throwing his ball of slime from hand to hand. 'There's millions o' girls out there on buses just like that. Millions. We'll never see her again.'

As they reached the outside door of the tenement Ronnie handed Will the slime and dug out his keys.

'Anyway, ye can't, ye know that,' he said, unlocking the door. 'The whole operation is completely confidential. Got tae be, or we're buggered.'

They felt their way through the dark inside corridor, and Will said, 'I wouldn't have tae tell her about it.'

Ronnie stopped for a moment. 'So what would ye say tae her?'

Will had no answer to that.

Ronnie went straight to Bruce's cage and let him out on the floor. Bruce didn't miss Ronnie while he was away, he had his own business to be getting on with, but it was important to keep up a routine.

'I'm goin' tae get a phone in here,' Ronnie said.

'A telephone?'

'Aye, fer phone calls an' things. Come an' look at this.' Ronnie opened his wardrobe. There was a lot of stuff in there – complete sets of Japanese soldiers and Ghurkas, a bag of toy cars, the monopoly set, stacks of *Biker* magazine, and his clothes. And there were two cardboard boxes from the grocer's, one labelled 'Money' and one labelled 'Misc'. Ronnie pulled them out to show Will, and transferred a necklace which had got into the money box by mistake.

'I won't touch that lot though,' Ronnie said, 'I'm no' breakin' the rules. I've been savin' up fer it anyway.' That was partly true.

Will didn't seem very impressed. He hardly looked in the boxes. He walked towards the window, and said, 'I'm goin' up tae the bus station.'

He hadn't even been listening. Ronnie walked right up to Will and looked him in the face. Will held something out to him. It was the slime. He snatched it from Will's hand, disgusted.

'Dae you know what the penalty for armed robbery is?' Ronnie shouted. 'Have you any idea?' Will was just watching him. He had

50

no idea. 'It's twelve years. Twelve years. And assault. Threatening behaviour . . .' He struggled to think of other charges.

Will said, 'Not wearing a crash helmet.'

Ronnie looked down at his hand. The slime was dribbling off in a long stream which had nearly reached the carpet, and he bent over to save it. Will was still watching him. Maybe he had been a bit harsh. There was no point in over-reacting, especially with friends.

'Will please,' he said. 'No going into the bus station.' Will nodded. 'No speaking to anybody except her. No telling her who you are. No mention that I even exist. Right?'

Will was still nodding. He started to go for the door, but Ronnie stopped him.

'Wait.'

Ronnie dug in the chest of drawers and brought out a small pink tube. It had a label on the side which said 'Pettifer's Ointment – guaranteed relief from shingles, scabies, eczema, psoriasis, warts, and other conditions of the skin.' He had been in the chemist getting cotton wool for Bruce's nest, and it had caught his eye. He threw the tube to Will.

Will looked at the label, grinned at Ronnie, and disappeared through the door.

The office was in chaos when Baird arrived. There were bus passengers all over the place, and there wasn't room to swing a trout fly. They were clogging up the privies, the corridors, the interview rooms, even the operations room. At least three officers were crowded round a pair of young ladies in a corner, there was a man in a baseball hat sitting on the sergeant's desk, another chattering away to a stenographer in a language Baird had certainly never heard before, and on the artist's desk there was a woman with blue hair leafing through what looked like a book of stills from horror films.

'No, I think it's more like the Lon Chaney one,' Baird heard her say as he forged a channel through the room. Sergeant Mackintosh stopped him by the filing cabinets, pointing to the back, and sure enough there was the American, chattering away outside Baird's office on what looked like one of those fangled cordless telephones. Baird headed for his open door, nodding as he passed, and the American waved a podgy hand in mid-sentence.

The juniors were larking about inside. He had been landed with Dunn and Harley since the start of this case. They were the new breed of detective, and he knew what that meant. They were playing basketball with a ball of paper. Baird shouted as he hung up his coat and deerstalker.

'Quiet. Cut the racket! Cut – the – racket.' They sat quietly. Baird pulled out his glasses and removed the slip of paper from the book he'd been carrying, *Freshwater Fish in Scotland*. He addressed the juniors.

'Now I've got a telex here from the Secretary of State for Scotland.' They looked blankly up from their desks by the window. 'The Scottish Secretary,' Baird said. He began to read: '"Advise utmost expedition in apprehending highwaymen. Potential political hot potato."' He glanced up, amused. 'How about that, eh?' No reaction. Baird read on. '"Swift action and low profile imperative. Ends."' There was a time when crime work was not a matter of impertinent telexes from politicians, and junior detectives being posted into your private office when your back was turned.

Baird surveyed the room. His 'Fish-spotter's Guide' poster was entirely obscured by a map of Scotland which the juniors had stuck up, with two red flags piercing the remote Highlands. Beside it were identikit pictures of a clown and a wolfman. Baird smiled. What could you do?

'Low profile,' he said.

'Low profile,' said Dunn, writing it down on the pad in front of him. Harley caught sight of him and wrote it down as well.

'Imperative,' Baird said.

'Imperative,' said Dunn and Harley.

'Anyway,' Baird tossed the telex down on his desk, pulling his jumper off as he spoke, 'what it comes down to is these lads have shanghaied two coachloads of what is considered a prize import in this country –' the last few words merged into a muffled blur as the jumper passed over his head – 'and we are instructed to nip this in the bud before they do any further damage to our relations with our friends from abroad.'

He made a careless nipping gesture with his thumb and first finger, and caught sight of Dunn nipping back at him. Bloody irritating. Baird sat down, stretching out his legs in front of him.

'Liaison with the bus companies you know about, and you should have no language difficulties there,' he said. 'Forensic and back-up are available through me, as is Interpol.'

The juniors were still watching him, like kids in a classroom. Through the glass partition from the main room he could see the American pacing up and down, still talking on the contraption, glancing into the office every so often. He was dressed in a well-pressed light suit and tie, and had a nasty red rash on one of his cheeks.

'Now this investigation is taking place in an international framework,' Baird said, 'and we will be assisted in our work by a gentleman from Central America – ah, from the American Central Intelligence Agency, who I shall introduce to you now.'

The American waved through the partition at Baird's expectant look and wandered in the door, holding his telephone to his ear. He smirked at the juniors, wrinkling up his little piggy eyes.

'Mister Fritz Bender,' Baird said.

Bender raised his free hand, still listening to the telephone. 'Hi!' he said.

Harley leaned over towards Dunn. 'Oh Christ,' he said, 'it's the Man from Uncle.'

– 8 –

Will felt fuddled. He walked up and down the bus station yard, stared through the windows of the waiting-room, shuffled several times round the staff building, and stamped about on the pavement outside. In the end he sat on a bench outside the waiting-room, waiting. All the doors were locked, and there didn't seem to be anybody about at all.

He walked home just as the pubs were coming out, dodging groups of drunks in the city centre. He looked at everybody's face, just in case, and into cars, and into any lit-up windows he went past. It took him two hours to get back to Wester Hailes. Even as he walked through the estate he kept an eye out for anybody else on the streets, or looking out of their window. Nothing was impossible.

He slept late next morning, and Mother said Father was on the warpath.

After a cup of coffee, Will went to his wardrobe and selected his very best clothes. He had a dark purple shirt with a big collar, his old smart flared brown trousers, and the blue jacket with the big lapels. The jacket was a bit too small, but it didn't show badly unless it was buttoned up. He put on his only tie, a flowery one that used to be Father's, and borrowed Isla's comb again to do his hair.

There was a bit at the top of his head that just wouldn't lie down, whatever he did. Isla said it was because his brain was curly. He tried plastering it down with water, and looked in the bathroom mirror. It stuck up like a loose wire. He didn't have any hats.

He told Mother he was going to the Job Centre, and caught a bus into town.

The bus station was much busier, and Will looked carefully round a wall from the main street outside. Buses were coming and going all the time, and people bustled past him in every direction. Most of the buses looked much the same as the one they'd just done. Will started to examine each face, working from the main street inwards, and then stopped. Police.

There were two of them, talking to a bus driver at the door of a coach. One of them was holding a small piece of paper, a photograph, Will thought, and the driver was nodding at it. Will shrunk back behind the outside wall on the pavement. They couldn't see him there, and he could still watch about a quarter of the bus station. He started examining faces again.

No matter how fast he made his eyes move, he couldn't see

every face. There were thousands of people, getting on and off buses, waiting in queues, going into and coming out of the offices, or the waiting-room, or the toilets. He caught a glimpse of a girl in the dark red courier's uniform, and rushed forward to see better, but she was blonde, with a big nose.

A car hooted – he realised he was standing in the middle of the road, and jumped back to the wall. The policemen had moved to another part of the yard, and they were showing the photograph to a group of brightly-dressed people standing by a pile of luggage. The people were laughing.

Will decided to concentrate on the girls in uniform. There were two or three of them, standing talking in a group beside a coach, and he saw another one just disappearing into the office building.

It was a grey day, and Will was cold. He buttoned up his jacket and turned the collar up. He couldn't move his arms properly, but he would unbutton it if anything happened. People were staring at him as they passed in and out of the bus station entrance, and he pretended he had a little pad and pen to write down bus numbers. Bus spotting.

As time went on, he saw several more of the couriers in the yard, but he was always disappointed. His knees were tired, and he squatted down against the wall, still peering round the corner. He pulled Ronnie's tube of ointment from his fingers, and read the instructions. 'Not to be taken internally,' it said. He dabbed a bit on his fingers. It was pink and greasy, but it didn't smell of anything. He dabbed some more on, just to be sure.

It must have been around lunch time when it started to rain. Will slumped down on the ground, wrapping the jacket around him as tightly as he could.

Margot had only met Mr Illingworth once since she'd started as a courier, and that was in connection with the Cold War incident.

About three months after she started working for the company, a young man locked himself into the coach toilet on a tour of the Trossachs and refused to come out until he was granted political asylum. The situation was desperate because they were a hundred miles from Edinburgh with seventy passengers who had just had a pub lunch. In the end Margot persuaded him to come out by pretending to be an agent from the Home Office.

When he emerged the man soon realised who she really was, even though she was wearing the driver's overcoat, but by that time there was a queue for the toilet. The man insisted on leaving the bus and ran away across the fields in the direction of Loch Vennacher. The passengers were very excited about the whole thing. When they got back to Edinburgh the reporters and television cameras appeared and somebody did ring the Home Office, but it turned out the man was a student doing a stunt for a new Communist group. He wandered into a Perthshire village police station the next day and said he was lost.

Margot was called into Mr Illingworth's office and was told off for not calling the police immediately, although she had been in the middle of the mountains when the man defected. But Margot had the impression it was the 'bloody reds' that Mr Illingworth was really annoyed at. She didn't feel so lucky this time.

She was told to come in on her day off, and she sat waiting outside Mr Illingworth's office for half an hour. Everybody passing wanted to know about the robbers, and she was happy to tell them, though she worried when they laughed too loudly. The couriers were planning to have a lottery on who got robbed next.

When Mr Illingworth opened his door and showed her into his office, Margot knew the reds weren't getting the blame. He didn't say a word until she was sitting on a little chair in front of his great wooden desk, and he was behind it. Then he put on his reading glasses, shifted some papers about, and looked at her.

'You've seen Superintendent Baird?' he said.

'Yes,' said Margot. 'A nice man.'

She hadn't been sure whether Mr Baird was amazed or amused by her story, until they got talking about the Age of Chivalry. He was a very nice man. But, he said, the robbers would have to pay.

Mr Illingworth looked gravely at her. He sniffed, and twiddled his thumbs on the desk in front of him.

'They tell me you are a nice enough girl,' he said. 'You do your job well, you're patient with the customers, and you know the country. You've had a fine record since the last – incident.' He paused, and his thumbs became still. 'What went wrong?'

Margot hesitated. She was trying to take it seriously, but it was ridiculous. She smiled, sitting forward.

'You see,' she said, 'I've always had a thing about wolves!' She laughed good humouredly. Mr Illingworth's face didn't move a muscle, and she stopped. 'Mr Illingworth, they had a gun,' she said. 'You could hardly ask me to tackle two masked gunmen.'

He looked down at an open file on his desk. Margot leaned forward as far as she could. There was a photograph of her when she joined the company, when her hair was longer. Underneath it was a lot of writing, but she couldn't make out any of it. Mr Illingworth took a pen from its stand in the roof of a small silver tour-coach that stood on his desk, and wrote something on the file.

'You've been with us two years now,' he said, 'and frankly, whatever Superintendent Baird may say, we're left with a busful of irate clients on our hands, and you're half the cause of their worry.'

It was so unfair. Margot had never done anything that would make the passengers unhappy, even if she had very much felt like it sometimes. She started to complain, but he interrupted her, waving his finger.

'I'm not going to threaten you. I'm quite sure you are aware of all the possibilities open to the company.'

He slid out of his chair and came round to the front of the desk, perching on the edge of it so that his leg was almost touching her knee. She didn't like that at all.

His voice became quiet and sympathetic, and he took off his glasses and put them on the desk behind him.

'We're not an unfeeling company,' he said. Margot shivered. 'I can understand a pretty young girl, in high spirits –' he put his hand gently on her arm, just at the elbow – 'getting carried away.'

Margot jumped up briskly, moving backwards towards the door as she talked, and trying to keep cheery. A year and a half on the buses had taught her that manners were very important at times like this.

'Yes, well we all get carried away sometimes,' she said. 'But – duty first! The passenger is always right!' She had almost reached the door. She groped for the handle behind her back. 'Although I must tell you we had a Canadian lady on the Inverarden run last week who swore she was Bonny Prince Charlie!' The door was open.

Illingworth just sat on the edge of the desk, looking at her. He shouted as she backed out of the door.

'I expect flawless reports about you, courier! Flawless!'

It had been raining for about an hour when Will decided on a new plan. The police station. She would be at the police station. She might even have been arrested to give vital evidence or reconstruct what had happened. All he had to do was wait outside the police station, and sooner or later she would appear.

He went up the public steps to the bridge joining the main street to the shopping centre and the bus station offices. There was a conveyor-belt there like a flat escalator, for people with luggage. You just stood on it, and it moved you. Will stepped on.

He was leaning against the rail, going at about four miles an hour, when he looked up and saw the girl coming down the walkway towards him. He struggled with the buttons of his jacket, smearing pink cream down the front of it. She was getting closer all the time, walking in the opposite direction to the conveyor-belt. He pulled a miniature brandy bottle from his pocket, drained it down, and then stuffed four extra-strong mints in his mouth. It was her.

She hadn't noticed him. Will began to walk backwards at four miles an hour so that he wouldn't be carried away.

'Excuse me,' he said.

She looked at him curiously and stopped. 'I'm sorry?'

She was even prettier than before. She wasn't in uniform, and she looked great. Will stared at the perfect nose, chewing desperately to clear his mouth, and said it again.

'Excuse me.'

She looked at him blankly for a moment. Then she smiled. She smiled at him!

He blinked, and she started to move away. Will walked backwards as hard as he could, but when he tried to speak all that came out was a sound like a dog barking.

'I'm sorry,' she said, 'I'm in a bit of a hurry.'

'Please?' said Will.

She hesitated, and then she started moving closer to him. There was a little raindrop on her chin. She was lovely. She tilted her head as if she'd caught sight of something and stared into his eyes.

Will suddenly thought of Ronnie, and for a moment his legs stopped going backwards so fast. A crowd of men with suitcases brushed past him, and he nearly lost his balance.

'I know you,' she said.

'No ye don't,' said Will very quickly. 'Oh no, quite impossible, no no no, some sort o' mistake.'

She smiled at him again, and turned to go. What was happening? Will scrabbled in his pocket.

'Would ye like a mint?' he said. She whirled round and looked straight into his face.

'I do know you, don't I?'

Will's legs were getting tired. He waved a mint with bits of fluff on it. 'Extra strong.'

She seemed sure of herself now, and almost impatient. 'What do they call you?'

Will shook his head. 'Ye don't know me, my name's Will and ye've never seen me before, an' I've got a very bad hand.' He held it up to show her. She tightened her coat and started to move off, still with a small smile. Two girls on roller skates whizzed past.

'Maybe I'll see you again then Will,' she said.

Will's legs had frozen to a halt, and he was being carried away. Bus passengers and shoppers bumped past him with their bags, staring. He could see her back as she walked briskly away in the opposite direction. She had lovely legs. Will stood up on tiptoe.

'I hold up buses!' he yelled.

They ran through the rain outside the shopping centre and caught a bus. Not a tourist bus, a double-decker Edinburgh Corporation Transport number 26, heading towards Newhaven. Her name was Margot, and she lived in Newhaven.

The upper deck of the bus was completely empty. Will watched the rain lashing down on the city streets. He couldn't decide if he wanted to look out of the window, because she was right there beside him, or look at her, because she was right there beside him.

He wanted to know everything. 'What was it then?' he said.

She looked straight at him, smiling that magic smile. He wanted to kiss it. It was only about eight inches away.

'Your big bonny blue eyes, Mr Wolf,' she said.

Will began to answer, but the bus had stopped and suddenly there were wet kids everywhere, shouting and screaming. A woman appeared at the top of the stairs, yelling 'Three to a seat . . . three to a seat!' The bus was hotching with wee girls. 'This one's bagged,' yelled one, leaping into the seat behind Will and Margot. 'I'm soakin',' screamed another, joining her, and a third crammed in, crying 'three to a seat'. A tired-looking man with a bus ticket longer than his arm stumbled up the stairs, and the bus moved off again. The girl sitting right behind Will gave a long desperate wail. 'I'm burstin'!'

Margot looked as if she was enjoying the chaos. She was laughing.

'They're grey,' said Will.

Margot looked closely at him. 'No they're not, they're blue.'

Her lovely eyes were deep, dark brown. 'Is that better?' Will said.

'I'm burstin',' the little girl whimpered.

Margot looked very gravely at Will, and he fidgeted with his hand for a minute. It was still pouring down outside.

'Why did you find me?' she said suddenly. He didn't know what to say. She looked at her feet.

'I've still got your flowers, it's the best present I've ever had,' she said. Will was happy. He was sure they would have been dead by now.

'I'm burstin',' the girl cried.

Margot was frowning. 'Are you trying to get me to work for you on the buses?'

'No,' said Will. How could she think that? 'No.' She smiled. He stared out the window, fidgeted, and looked back at her. 'Ye won't tell anyone, will ye?'

Margot shook her head gravely.

The little girl piped up louder than ever. 'I'm really burstin'!'

Will smiled at Margot, and she smiled back. He felt great.

'Ye know, I could fair go a pee mysel',' he said.

At Newhaven they left the bus and darted through the rain along the concrete foreshore. Margot sat in an old boat that lay on its side by the sea wall, while Will went behind the rusty wreck of an old crane.

'I really thought she was goin' tae make it,' he said, settling down beside her in the shell of the boat. 'I really did.'

They watched the rain skittering along the wet concrete shelf where the sea met the land. Will felt relaxed with Margot, which was something he didn't usually feel. She liked him. 'Say some more,' he said.

She grinned. 'Are you looking for flattery?' Will made a face of yes-but-you-shouldn't-ask. Margot seemed to understand. They watched the rain. They were sitting close beside each other.

'I never met a robber before,' she said. Margot was a real person, she knew about life.

'I just wonder if it's quite right, the whole thing,' he said.

'It's like Rob Roy, isn't it?' Margot said. Will tried to remember who Rob Roy was. 'Rob Roy,' she said, looking at him strangely. Will nodded, and she went on.

'They called him the Highland Robin Hood, you know, three hundred years ago. We used to read the stories, me and my dad. I thought Rob Roy was better than Batman or Superman or any of them.'

Will was beginning to understand. 'Oh Batman's good,' he said.

'But real people are best. I'm going to have to update my commentary now because of you. But I don't mind at all.' She shook her head. 'It's better, because you're still alive.'

When Will really liked something, his face collapsed. His mouth hung open, his eyes went all glassy, and his neck felt like jelly. He couldn't help himself.

'Well, you were a minute ago,' Margot said. Will grinned.

− 9 −

Ronnie was a wanted man, and he loved it. Stinker Todd, the careers man, used to say that finding the right job was simply a matter of defining your talents, channelling them through your interests, and matching them to the correct area of expression. Good old Stinker, Ronnie had found the perfect match.

Planning was easy. There were hundreds and hundreds of tour coaches, every day, touring on thousands of miles of roads in the Highlands. After a few weeks Ronnie took the train to Glasgow and visited the tourist office there, and he came back with three carrier-bags full of new timetables for his collection. Rich pickings.

Choosing the right bus was an art. Most of them had to travel on the quiet B-roads for some of the time, so it was a matter of picking an area Will and Ronnie hadn't worked before, and preferably a company they hadn't hit. It was best not to show favouritism.

Ronnie soon learnt to avoid the all-foreign tours, because of communication problems. There was one bus they stopped in a glen in the Cairngorms, a luxury bus with observation windows in the roof, and it wasn't a great success. The courier couldn't get the hang of it at all. She was a snooty wee girl with dark skin, and she shook her head when Ronnie jumped up the steps and told her the form. She turned to the passengers and said something, and then she turned to Ronnie and Will and babbled non-stop for about three minutes. Will kept telling Ronnie she was saying 'Put the horse in the stable', but it wasn't any language Ronnie had ever heard.

He showed her the gun, he showed her the puffer, and he brought a tuppenny bit out of his pocket and put it into Will's haversack. Nothing. She produced a big leaflet with pictures of the emergency exits on the bus, and how the air-conditioning worked. 'Welcome to Scotland', it said at the top. He tried again, showing her a newspaper cutting that he had in his pocket. Nothing. In the end they just had to puff her and leave the bus.

A respectable hold-up took about seven and a half minutes. Ronnie had started timing them on the new calculator watch that came from a Scottish Lochs Tour bus. They could do it in five if there was a chance of traffic on the road, but that was a hasty job, and difficult to do with style. Ten was plain inefficiency.

It was impossible to guarantee against traffic on the road while they were working. The best places were high up, so that you could see far down the road before you started, and check it was clear. Twice, cars came up behind when they were in the middle of a job, and just went straight past. Then one time in the Grampian Mountains they were about half way through on a day-excursion bus, and another tour bus came up and parked right behind them. Will and Ronnie stopped what they were doing, and waited to see what would happen. Tourists were pouring off the other bus peering in the windows at the clown and wolfman, and then they started taking pictures of them. Will finished his collection, and then the two of them jumped off and did another collection on the passengers from the second bus. It was a good day.

There was the occasional joker who tried to sit on his money or something like that, and somebody would always bring out his credit cards, but they had no real problems.

Over the weeks, the bus passengers seemed to be getting nicer on every trip. A lot of them knew who the clown and the wolfman were from the papers or the telly, and they were usually quite pleased to see them. Honoured, even. One wifey on a luxury coach took a real shine to Will. She was all make-up and low neckline, and she practically tried to give him her clothes for the collection. They looked like expensive clothes too, silk and stuff, but Will stopped her.

Will agreed that it was important not to take things for granted. If they got too big-headed people wouldn't like them at all. Early on they stopped taking wedding-rings and engagement rings, and if people looked too miserable they didn't collect too much from them. It was a fair system.

The police were a problem. Once, Will and Ronnie had just got on a bus when they heard a police siren, a long way away. They left immediately, and they never even saw the police car. But it was important to be sure of getting away safely, and so Ronnie invented the spray-stop.

The principle was simple. They stuck to single-track roads, and stopped the buses between trees or rocks or walls where it was impossible to overtake. Then when Will had made the collection, Ronnie went to the back of the bus and opened the engine.

One of the big sellers in the joke shop was the streamer spray, an aerosol can which shot out long strings of sticky luminous stuff. Kids bought them for spraying at teachers or messing up the outside of people's houses. If you sprayed a full can into the engine, concentrating on the spark plugs, a bus was buggered. It would take a good half hour to clean it up and get it going, and meanwhile Will and Ronnie had the road to themselves.

Ronnie liked having his faithful sidekick around, but he needed to keep him in line. He didn't enjoy it, but he had to be strict with Will about the lassie from the bus company. There was a lot at stake. Will hadn't mentioned the lassie again.

It was a question of good management. Will got strange ideas into his head that had nothing to do with running a serious business. On one bus he sat down beside a wifey at the back and started chatting away to her, and when they left the bus he took the wifey's big white hat with ribbons on it, and put it on top of his wolfman head. Then he insisted on wearing the hat for the whole getaway. It looked ridiculous.

It was worse with the hitchhikers. They were just coming away from a bus when Will made Ronnie stop at the side of the road. There were two men wearing rucksacks and carrying a big sign that said 'Inverness', and Will wanted to give them a lift. Will was young, though – he would learn.

Baird had had enough of the press.

He didn't mind giving an interview at the end of a case, when the work was all over. Twenty years ago, when he'd picked up Harry Niven, they'd called him Basher Baird, the man who smashed the gangland syndicates. He could handle the fuss then, though the boys in the office stuck 'Basher' signs on his door.

But Harry Niven had been a real crook. A real, nasty, big-time crook, who did a lot of very bad things to people, like killing them. And now here was Basher Baird, hirpling about all over the entire bloody country to pick up two juveniles on a motorcycle. And the press was having a field day.

It could take years. Dunn and Harley's map had six red flags on it. The motorbike kids were fair travelling, and they could be coming from Edinburgh, Glasgow, Inverness, Aberdeen – anywhere. The hold-ups had started at a rate of one a week, and tailed off to about one every ten days or fortnight, but there was no pattern. They were using a cheap, standard Japanese bike, the manufacturers said there were about twenty thousand in the country. The number-plates were untraceable. They didn't exist. And the front one was a different number from the back. Identikit pictures of clowns and wolfmen had gone to police stations and post offices all over the country. The Guild of Circus Performers had complained.

Patrol cars from all the Highland stations had stepped up their attention to B-roads, and never seen a whisker of them. The Secretary had ruled out the question of arms on the buses, thank the Lord. Thirty uniformed officers from the Inverness station spent six hours tracing a motorbike treadmark across open fields, fording a river, through a forest and down a mountainside. The track ran down to the edge of Loch Moy, and disappeared straight into the water.

Officers with waders searched the area near the shore with sticks till darkness, and frogmen quartered the Loch. Three days later there was another hold-up, on the other side of the Highlands. Smart-alec wee buggers.

Baird could feel himself being backed into a corner. The case was a dead duck, and it should never have been his case anyway. Six months away from his retirement, he knew who would take the fall if the kids weren't caught soon. Not a great way to go.

He leant back in his chair, staring idly at the wall behind him, where a twenty-four-pound salmon was mounted in a glass case. 'J. Baird – River Tay – 7 Sept. 1959', said the little plaque. Either way, in six months time he would be sitting on the shore of Loch Lubnaig with a rod in his hand, as happy as Larry. He decided to let the Press Office deal with all enquiries.

'You, eh, thinking, Mr Baird?' Bender said. The American was grinning across at him. Baird smiled back. The podgy wee runt had somehow managed to insert himself right into Baird's office, in the spirit of international co-operation. Bender sat at Harley's desk now, and Harley and Dunn had to share a desk, like schoolchildren.

Bender seemed to be tied up with his own business most of the time, whatever that was. He was endlessly gabbing on his cordless phone, a ridiculous gadget that didn't ring like a normal telephone, but whooped a piercing electronic banshee noise. Baird was sure he had heard Bender use the word 'divorce' more than once, but it was difficult to say because the American paced about with the phone as he talked, and huddled into corners. Sometimes it sounded as if he was talking to his superiors in Virginia, but most of the time it wasn't clear what he was doing.

Often Bender just sat behind his desk, scratching at his rash – some sort of allergic reaction to the mystery powder the motorbike kids had thrown. It was Baird's habit, in moments when he had nothing else to do, to browse through the small library of fishing almanacs which he kept in his locker, and it was always at those moments that Bender would choose to ask about Baird's investigations.

Baird tried sending him out with patrol cars as far away as possible, but Bender always came back twice as intent on knowing Baird's plan to catch the robbers. Dunn and Harley thought the American was a great sideshow, and sat snickering about him at the next desk, but he never paid them the slightest attention.

'Fine day,' Bender said. Baird looked out of the window. It was too hot for fish to be biting.

As he turned to the American there was a great banshee wail, and Bender scrabbled at the papers on his desk. Baird put his fingers in his ears.

'Where is it?' yelled Bender, thrashing through the files in front of him. The phone clearly wasn't there. Harley got up and started tugging at a drawer in Bender's desk. It wouldn't open. Dunn was sniggering, also with his fingers in his ears.

Bender was furious. 'It's my personal phone,' he shouted. 'I only left it for fifteen minutes. It was right there on the top.'

Harley crawled underneath the desk, trying to force the jammed drawer out from behind.

'It just kept ringing when you were away,' he said, squinting up from the level of Bender's knees. 'I couldn't switch it off.' He battered at the underside of the desk with a fist. 'It wasn't my idea to put it in the drawer.'

Baird stifled a smile. Bender was tugging furiously at the drawer handle. 'This could be an important call,' he said. Dunn spluttered.

Baird addressed Dunn as gravely as he could manage. 'Get a hammer.'

Space was becoming a problem. Ronnie bought two large rubbish bags, labelled them 'Cash' and 'Misc', and transferred the stuff from the cardboard boxes. The bags wouldn't fit in the wardrobe, so he left them out, turned their labels to the wall, and tied up their necks with bits of string. Then Mrs Denzler came in and lost her rag because he hadn't been putting out his rubbish.

She stood and watched as he carried the two bags out into the street and set them by the lamp-post, and then she asked for the rent. All the money was in the 'Cash' bag. Ronnie said things were very bad at the shop and he would have to pay her next week, and she left in a bad temper. He watched her to the end of the road and then went out and brought the bags back in.

They had £5,112, not counting the rent money and change. Ronnie tapped away at his calculator watch. They would be millionaires in forty-four years if they kept up the pace. So he spent a day going round the building societies, comparing interest rates and terms. They could get 13.7% interest, if only they could find some way of depositing the money without people getting suspicious.

The important thing with a business was not to stand still. Expansion was the key to creating wealth, Stinker Todd told his Business class, and he was right. Ronnie and Will were operating in a very specialised field, and what they needed was access to specialised resources and experience. Ronnie would have to make a plan.

– 10 –

Catholics were used to it. It was easy for them, thought Will. They were brought up to it. If he was Catholic he could probably get it over with just like that – 'Forgive me Ronnie, for I have sinned.'

Ronnie wasn't paying any attention. He was sitting cross-legged on the doorstep, pasting up the scrapbook on his knees. The scrapbook was almost full. Lately he had been going up to the railway station newsagent to buy all the foreign newspapers as well as the Scottish ones. 'Ladres "Highland" Fanno Un Casino', said the one Ronnie was just cutting out. They were famous all over the world.

It was a sunny afternoon, and Will leaned back against the

railings, watching Ronnie. There was no good reason why Ronnie should be angry about what Will had done.

Ronnie was smoking a big cigar, and he spoke to Will as he smeared glue on the back of a cutting.

'We should really try to get some better pictures of ourselves,' he said.

Will tried to imagine being Catholic. 'Ronnie?' he said.

Ronnie squinted up from the book, and when Will didn't say any more he passed the book over to him, pointing.

'That looks like a real person's face, that,' he said. 'I dinnae want anyone tae think I'm W. C. Fields.'

Will squinted at the cutting. It was a two-page spread, with maps of where they'd done the hold-ups, and a diagram of the inside of a bus. 'Bandit Country!' said the headline. There was a picture of an old man in a deerstalker hat, and underneath it said, 'Superintendent James Baird, who is co-ordinating the investigation, warned tourists to take the utmost care when travelling on the coaches.' Then there was a blurred picture of Will and Ronnie standing in their masks at the front of a bus. There was something familiar about the picture.

'Hey, I know who took that,' Will said. 'Remember the wee black wifey in the shades? She kept shouting cheese.'

Ronnie nodded, though he didn't look as if he remembered. Will stuck his nose right up against the picture.

'I always have my eyes shut in photos,' he said. The woman hadn't even been using a flash, but Will always blinked at the precise moment a camera went off. There was no such thing as a picture of Will with his eyes open.

Ronnie took the scrapbook back, puffed a long puff at his cigar, put it carefully back on the ground and started cutting out another article.

Will swallowed. He knew he'd feel better once he'd got it off his chest. 'Em,' he said.

Ronnie looked up and said, 'We could go up to the machine at the Post Office. Get it done properly.'

Will wondered what he meant.

'To send to the papers,' Ronnie said impatiently. He opened a page of the scrapbook and pointed at it. 'There's one of these here describes you as 'heavily bearded'.'

Will shut his eyes and turned his head in Ronnie's direction. 'Ronnie, I've got something to tell you.'

'Aye, me too,' Ronnie said quietly. Will opened his eyes. Ronnie was making a face and scratching his head.

'I had a bit of an accident,' he said. 'Well I forgot Bruce was lining his nest, and he was out while I was at the shop. He was on twenties.' He looked up at Will cautiously.

The rules about the money had been altered, what with buying maps and phrasebooks and scrapbooks and telephones and cigars and hundreds of newspapers. Will and Ronnie had even stuck on false moustaches from the joke shop and driven sixty miles on the motorbike to Berwick, where they had a steak dinner with creamed potatoes, onion rings, chocolate milkshakes and brandy before driving home. But they couldn't spend much, and Will didn't care. Money wasn't everything.

'How much?' he said.

Ronnie scratched his head again, looking up at Will from under his elbow. 'About two hundred.'

Will shrugged. 'Oh well, that's all right.'

Ronnie looked pleased. He collected up the newspapers and the scrapbook and disappeared into the flat, shouting for Will to come on. Will got up and went after him. 'Ronnie, there's something I've got to tell you,' he said.

He still hadn't told him by the time they got up to the Post Office. The moment hadn't arisen.

Ronnie had the masks in a carrier bag, and he clutched it tightly as they waited outside the automatic photo booth, with crowds milling around. There were people inside, getting their picture taken. They were making a lot of noise. Will counted eight legs crammed together underneath the curtain in the doorway.

Eventually two girls and two boys came out laughing, and Will and Ronnie went in and closed the curtain behind them. The eight legs were milling around outside now, but the booth seemed secure. It was like a confession box. They put the masks on, and Ronnie put a coin in the slot.

'Right, look tough,' he said. There was a flash.

Will said, 'Ronnie, ken the girl, Margot, the girl on the bus?' There was another flash. Will couldn't see Ronnie's face through his mask, and he blurted on. 'Well, ken I promised no' tae tell her, ken, who I was an' that?' There was another flash. Ronnie didn't say anything. 'Well, I did, really.' The camera flashed for the final time.

Will was happier than he'd ever been in the whole of his life, and he wished Ronnie wasn't so angry about it. Being angry wasn't going to help anything, and he tried very hard to persuade Ronnie that Margot wasn't a security risk.

They had to wait outside the photo booth for four minutes while the pictures were developed. Ronnie timed it on his new watch, and it took six. They huddled over the bit where the pictures came out in case anyone saw them, and Ronnie ground his teeth.

He was even angrier when he saw the pictures, though the first one was all right apart from Will having his eyes shut. Will said he was sorry, and left Ronnie to meet Margot at the bus station. He didn't like leaving Ronnie so angry, but it was arranged.

From the bus station Margot took Will to the Museum of Childhood in the High Street. He hadn't been there since he was little, but Margot said grown-ups weren't afraid to go to a place like that. It was full of children, though. Margot payed for them both at the door.

At first they had seen each other once or twice a week, and then on Saturdays and Sundays, and somehow they ended up being together just about every day. Margot liked doing things, visiting places and going for walks and making expeditions, and it was like being back at Saughton Junior again. Will had got quite good at doing nothing very much, and it was hard work changing, but it was worth it.

Margot was quite small, only just over five feet, so Will had to bend over and she had to stand on her tiptoes for a hug or

71

anything. She was twenty, which was a bit older than Will, but it wasn't a great problem. She didn't feel twenty. She had a little flat in Newhaven which she owned, at least she would do when she payed the mortgage on it, and she had prospects with the bus company, though she didn't know if she really wanted them.

She liked what Will and Ronnie did as well. She wasn't interested in the newspapers and the telly stuff, but she thought they were like heroes, making things exciting again. Will didn't want to talk about their plans and what they did, though. He knew Ronnie wouldn't like it. That was business. He and Margot never talked about the police, either.

Margot kept asking to meet Ronnie, which was impossible. Ronnie never even wanted to talk about Margot, and he wasn't interested in anything Will had to say about her, especially after he knew she knew about him. He didn't want her to exist. Ronnie was Will's best friend, and Will would always do the hold-ups with him, but he could never get Margot and Ronnie into the same room. It was like two different lives he had.

On the top floor of the museum there was a big red machine where you cranked a handle and looked in a wee window, and you saw moving pictures. Will put in ten pence and cranked the handle, and he saw a woman all wrapped up in a bandage, and someone dressed like a butler unwrapping her. If he cranked the handle slowly, it went in slow motion, and if he cranked it fast it looked like Laurel and Hardy. Margot leaned her arms on the other side of the machine, watching Will watching the pictures.

'I think you need a skite on the bum and someone to tell you what to do, Will Bryce,' she said. He didn't know why she said that, he was just innocently cranking the handle.

Will said, 'Do you think I'm good-looking?' It was best to ask questions like that while you were doing something else.

'I think you look like Mr Tatty,' Margot said. Mr Tatty was her name for Will when he wasn't wearing his best clothes. When he was wearing his best clothes he was Mr Smooth.

'Isla says I'm no' exactly a male model,' Will said. Isla had been getting angry with him for borrowing her comb all the time.

'Exactly not, I would have said, aye,' Margot said. She liked him very very much, she had said so.

Will kept on cranking the handle, and the bandage was coming off the woman so that bits of her were popping out now. He couldn't see what it had to do with childhood.

'This is rude,' he said.

Margot came round to his side of the machine. 'Let's see,' she said, pushing him out of the way.

Next they went on to the penny-in-the-slot machines. They had been adjusted to take tuppenny coins because of inflation, but they were exactly the same as Will remembered them. There was a Ghost House one where a man was sitting in his house and the table flew in the air and bats and ghosts appeared from out of the cupboards.

Then there was one of an execution, where Mary Queen of Scots put her head under the guillotine and had it chopped off into a basket. Will didn't like it as much as the ghost house, and while Margot was watching it he got his brooch out of his pocket. It was a small golden brooch with a flying man on it, and it had come from a woman on the second bus. Will ran it over his warts automatically, over and over.

A crowd of kids had gathered round the machine to watch the execution. A wee boy said 'She's English' to his friend as the knife blade rose up above Queen Mary's head.

'You know,' Will said to Margot, 'I've been rubbing with this stupid brooch for about three weeks now, and it hasn't made any difference at all.' Three weeks ago he'd had seven warts, two small, four medium and one large, and they were still exactly the same.

'That's what you get for listening to old wives' tales,' Margot said, still watching the machine.

'Maybe they'll spread all over me,' he said, 'like barnacles, and I'll have to have my bottom scraped.'

The guillotine came slamming down, and the head fell all bloody into the basket. The kids cheered. 'English wanker,' one of

73

them shouted at the corpse. Margot took Will by the arm and led him away from the machine, smiling up at him.

'Much easier to burn them off,' she said.

On Saturday they went shopping in Princes Street, and Margot bought Will a shirt. It was real cotton, and much better than all his nylon and polyester shirts, she said. Most of Will's shirts came out of Mother's Home Fashion Buyer catalogue as Christmas presents, but he was sure Mother would like this one. It had long sleeves and buttons on the cuffs.

They sat in the sun in Princes Street Gardens, and Margot tried to teach Will how to do backward somersaults. It was the first time he had been in the gardens since his resignation, but Margot didn't let him get worried about it. There was no sign of anyone clearing up the rubbish, but Will made sure that he collected up all the sweety papers and things beside him and put them in a bin. They even went down and got ice creams from Eddie's van, and Eddie was very nice to him, asking what he was up to now. Looking for a job, said Will. Eddie laughed.

The gardens were very busy with tourists, but Will and Margot sat on a quiet patch near the railway line. They stayed on towards the evening, and as most of the people drifted out to the main street Margot lay looking up at the sky and talked about her job.

'I hate the ones who throw up,' she said. 'But it's lovely up there. On Tuesdays we do the run up Strathalt, and we let them get out at the top of the Drumchrenan Pass.'

Will nodded, 'Aye I know, we've run through the forest.' Ronnie had gone completely berserk after one job and insisted on driving the bike right through the middle of the forest, straight through the trees, with no road or anything. They nearly crashed, and Ronnie skidded the bike and fell off. Then he spent the whole journey back complaining that his back was dislocated. But it was still a magic place.

Will said, 'It smells nice in there.'

'Scots Pine, two hundred years old, most of it,' Margot said. 'And the burns and things – have you tasted the water?'

Will was shocked. 'I always thought with the sheep and that . . .'

Margot sat up, bashing him hard on the shoulder so he nearly fell over. She was always beating him up.

'Will Bryce,' she said, 'it's the most beautiful water on God's earth.'

Will watched the last of the crowds straggling out through the gates of the park. They would be locking the place up for the night soon. Margot sat drawing pictures with her finger on the grass. She had lovely hands, with long thin fingers, not witchy with big nails or anything, and small palms about half the size of Will's. She had never had a wart in her life.

'My dad used to take me up to the Highlands when I was wee,' she said. 'When I started as a guide all I wanted to do was go back and learn everything about the hills.'

Will understood. 'Rob Roy,' he said.

Margot was still drawing on the grass. 'They're just old stories, the great heroes, I've told them so many times,' she said. 'I thought I must be getting old.'

Will shook his head, and she went on. 'But there's one legend that says the heroes aren't really dead, they're sleeping under the hills. And when Scotland really needs them, a magic trumpet sounds, and they wake up to help their native land.'

'Like ghosts?' Will said.

'Something like that. Do you believe in ghosts?'

Will thought for a minute. 'I don't know. I think I'm agnostic.'

Margot knew everything about the Highlands. 'The spirits are still there, among the mountains,' she said. 'They say that when the wind's really still you can hear them laughing in the glens, and plotting their return. It's like magic, it's like –' She turned to him at last. 'Do you know?'

Will nodded. He knew.

The Robin Hood business started by accident. They were doing a bus on a forest road very like Strathalt, and Ronnie had the idea of the Prime Minister's head.

It was just an ordinary full-head mask from the shop, but when you put it in the middle of the road and spread earth round the neck it looked like the Prime Minister buried in the ground. They waited behind a tree, and sure enough the coach came round the corner and screeched to a halt faster than any bus they'd ever stopped. There was chaos on the bus, with tourists crammed up against the front window all trying to get a good picture.

It took a while to get them calmed down, but it was a good day's work, and they left the bus a few minutes later with a good bagful of stuff. Ronnie booted the head away flying into the bushes, and they jumped on the bike and roared off.

They had a good ten miles to travel before they could change back to civilians, and it was as they were going through the village of Invergyle that Will noticed people behaving strangely. They were rushing out of their houses, out of shops, and out of the pub, and running about the street like madmen. Then he realised that with all the fuss about the head he'd forgotten to close the haversack, and there was money fountaining out all over the place.

Looking back he could see a gang of kids on roller skates skidding about on the road, catching fivers. Drunken men were flailing their arms, trying to grab notes as they floated past, and there was a wifey charging up and down with a fishing net. As the bike sped away Will could just make out a street cleaner sweeping up a great stack of money into his shovel and piling it into a yellow trolley.

Ronnie went mental. When they got back to the bedsit the haversack was nearly empty, with a few heavy bits of jewellery rattling about in the bottom. Will did his best to apologise, said Ronnie could have both shares of what was left, and promised never to let it happen again, but he couldn't get Ronnie out of his bad temper.

Then he was passing the newsagent the next day, and saw the headlines. He bought two copies of the paper, and took them to the joke shop. Ronnie humphed, and hummed, and then nodded his head slowly, and then grinned a big grin. He was back in a good temper. The paper had a big picture of them (a copy of the one decent photo-booth picture which Ronnie had posted anonymously to the BBC from Inverness) and the headline 'The Robin Hood Bandits'.

Ronnie thought it was great for the image. For the next bus he thought of an even better plan. The escape route took them directly past the huge Aberlong Old Folks' Home. As the bike raced past the low garden wall in brilliant sunshine, Will pulled wads and wads of notes out of the haversack, and flung them in the air.

He watched for as long as possible while the money showered down in the breeze on the lawn and window-sills of the home, landing on chess-players and ancient sunbathers out for the afternoon air. He could see one old man in a wheelchair looking straight up to the heavens, smiling at the different coloured banknotes that fell gently on his face.

– 11 –

Ronnie tried to concentrate on scraping the crusty bits off the bottom of Bruce's cage. His patience was running out. Will's ideas of how to run a business were becoming a positive liability. His first brainwave was to get involved in a personal affair with a member of the opposition, in direct defiance of Ronnie's instructions. The security risks were obvious to an idiot, and Will was using good working hours for liaisons. It was just amateur behaviour. Then he dumped an entire haversack of stuff – about £800 worth – in the middle of a Highland village by mistake. Ronnie had to admit there was good publicity potential in it, but when they did it deliberately Will dumped the whole lot yet again – another £800.

Ronnie put Bruce in a big cardboard box with some sawdust, and tipped the contents of the dirty cage out the window. It was a fine day. He had bought some supplies, including a £35 bag of cashew nuts from the wholesale grocer's and a bag of sawdust, and it was time Bruce had a spring-clean.

Will was moaning. He had now got it into his head that if you were going to give away free money, you had to distribute an equal amount to the entire population.

'I'm just sayin', it's no' fair,' he said. 'If ye went a bit slower maybe I could try an' hand out the money properly.'

Ronnie shook his head. He didn't know what he was going to do with him. He threw a handful of new sawdust into the cage, and transferred Bruce back to his clean home. Then he tipped the cardboard box out of the window and turned to Will, trying to keep calm.

'We're no' Santa Claus, Will,' he said. He started picking up the dirty clothes from the floor and throwing them into the cardboard box. 'It was a nice gesture, good for the image, fine. But I cannae have you frittering away our money like that. Dae you know how much you must have thrown oot?'

Will gave him a sulky look. 'You said it was a good idea,' he said. 'Bruce ate two hundred pounds.'

That was too much. Ronnie whipped round, waving his finger in Will's face.

'Dinnae you make insinuations about him,' he shouted. 'You've got your friends, I've got mine. Where do you get the money to buy ten billion cups of tea for you and your friend? Eh?'

Will had been taking several pounds from the 'Cash' bag every week, and Ronnie knew it went on tea. He'd seen Will waiting in the Canon Street cafe. It couldn't go on.

'It's not that many,' Will said.

Ronnie was angry. 'You're breaking the rules,' he said. 'You're using our money to fraternise, and now you want to give the rest away.'

When they were trying to decide what they could do with the money weeks before, Will had suggested that since they couldn't spend it, why didn't they give it all to some charity? He wanted to adopt one thousand black babies in Africa. Great business.

'I don't know what's happened to you,' Ronnie shouted. 'Where are you all the time?'

He went to Bruce's cage and started feeding Bruce cashew nuts from the sack. Bruce took them from his fingers one by one, and gradually Ronnie realised he wasn't picking them out of the sack anymore, but taking them one by one from Will's hand as Will passed them to him. Will looked confused.

'I'm not fraternising,' he said. 'She isn't . . .'

His face changed as Ronnie watched, and he was obviously trying to cheer up.

'Are we going up North again soon?' he said, nodding his head.

Ronnie knew he didn't really mean it. He probably wouldn't want to go at all, if Ronnie didn't tell him to. Will was changing. There was a certain age people reached and pop! – everything about them just collapsed into boringness. Will would probably be getting married soon, and he certainly wouldn't invite people like Ronnie to the wedding.

Will had always been Ronnie's friend. Maybe Ronnie should have been planning to hire special people to kidnap Will and de-brainwash him, but he couldn't be bothered. He had a business to be getting on with, and he could always use an extra pair of hands, for the moment anyway. What he couldn't put up with was Will pretending that he had any idea of what was what.

Ronnie wiped the cashew-nut grease from his fingers on to his jeans, and smiled a fake smile. He said, 'Have ye had some more constructive ideas about the business then?'

Will shook his head seriously. 'No, no, not at all, no,' he said. He was watching Ronnie very carefully, and in an instant he was nodding. 'Aye, aye, well yes I have.'

Ronnie just stared at him and let him blunder on.

'Well,' said Will, 'I was thinking, we could wear different masks, you know, throw them off the trail.' He looked down thoughtfully and his face brightened up. 'And we could put some different stuff in the puffer, just for a change, perfume or something.' Will looked pleased with himself now. 'Aye, we could have a nice puffer for people we liked.'

Ronnie didn't say anything. He just stared. Slowly Will's expression faded until he was looking down and fidgeting at his hand. He tried to smile.

'Only joking,' he said.

Ronnie remembered the girl courier from the second bus, of course. She was a pretty enough lassie. She simply had no part in the scheme of things. She was dangerous, and Ronnie could see how she was already damaging the business.

You got what you wanted in life, if you really really wanted it. But you had to be single-minded about it. Ronnie wanted to have his cake, and Will wanted to eat it.

Once when he was getting a bus to the joke shop, he saw them. They were in Princes Street Gardens, trying to do somer-saults. They were holding hands and laughing, as if they didn't have a care. Ronnie didn't watch. He wasn't interested.

There had been a few girls he'd liked at the home, but most of them didn't like him very much, and he was usually too busy with other stuff anyway. He wasn't interested in the romantic rubbish. There came a time in a man's life when he had to decide what was more important to him – his dedication to his work or his personal life, and Ronnie had chosen. Someday when he wasn't so busy he might have time for things like girlfriends.

Ronnie stayed late in the shop more and more after Will started having his affair. He didn't do the accounts or sort the stock or update the ordering much, he usually just sat on a chair behind the counter, smoking, and thinking. He could blow great smoke rings now, and put a small one through the middle of a big one, and hoop them over the light bulb, and all sorts.

One night he dozed off sitting in the chair. He hadn't been sleeping very well. He was woken by a tapping at the door, and he couldn't see who it was in the darkness outside. He stretched and stood up, and stumbled over to the door. It was a hot night, and he felt horrible and sweaty.

When he got near the door he realised it was her. She was wearing an overcoat now, but it was the same pretty face and wavy brown hair. Her face was pressed right up against the glass, peering in, and she knocked lightly. Ronnie didn't know what to do. She was waving now, she had seen him. He shouted out.

'You're smudging the door.' It wasn't true. She didn't look as if she had greasy skin, and she wasn't spotty. She stopped waving and spoke back, though her voice sounded so far away through the door that he could hardly hear it.

'Is Will there?'

Ronnie walked up to the door. This was Will's fault. Ronnie wasn't going to get involved. He just didn't want anything to do with it.

'Will who?' he shouted. She shouted back faintly, trying to explain. It looked quite windy outside.

'Will Bryce. I'm his friend.' She pointed to the lock on the door. 'Can I come in?'

It wasn't fair. It wasn't part of the plan, he had to draw the line somewhere. She was speaking to him like he was an idiot. 'Will Bryce,' Ronnie shouted, scratching his chin. 'Now is he related to wee Tommy Bryce that used to work down the bottle factory?' In some ways he really didn't know Will at all any more, and he didn't want to. He had to think about himself.

She was anxious, sweeping her hair away from her eyes with her hand. She had smiled a bit at first, but she'd stopped now.

'Are you Ronnie?' drifted through the door. She didn't have a very loud voice. 'You're his friend Ronnie,' she shouted. 'Let me in!'

He was no Ronnie she knew. He was getting impatient, and he didn't bother shouting this time, so he couldn't tell if she even heard him. He pointed to the lock.

'The door's locked. It's shut. There's no Ronnie here.'

She banged on the door with the palms of her hands, looking worried. She seemed to think everybody had gone crazy.

'I know about it. I know. I'm a friend,' she shouted.

Ronnie unlocked the door and opened it about a foot. The wind whistled into the shop and blew a paper off the counter. She looked relieved, smiling again, though her eyes were watery as if she was nearly crying. She put a hand on the door to squeeze in. She had a nice face. He knew her name was Margot.

She was looking straight in his eyes, waiting. For a moment Ronnie forgot himself, and all he wanted to do was to bring her in the shop and make her feel better. She needed him. Then a gust of wind snatched at the door, and he remembered automatically. He avoided looking at her eyes.

'I can't,' he said. 'Ronnie's dead. Passed away. Very very sad. I've got to finish the accounts.'

He closed the door as quickly as he could and locked it again without looking. Then he walked straight to the back room, where he switched off the main shop lights. Through the darkness he could still see a shape standing at the door. He messed around tidying the stock shelves, and when he looked again, she had gone.

It wasn't raining in the cemetery. It was a bit breezy, but the sky was clear and blue. Ronnie wondered if that was a bad omen. It was the first time he had been in weeks, and he felt guilty about that, but things had been very hectic. Since the business got off the ground he hadn't really been that bothered about going.

In fact, as he walked down among the battered gravestones, he wasn't at all sure why he'd gone today. He was in a bad mood. He'd had to take a lot of career decisions lately, and he hadn't been getting much sleep.

There were a few people around, one or two sitting or standing by stones, a gang of kids chasing and yelling, and the occasional couple, hand in hand. Ronnie pretended he was just wandering about too. He didn't want any of them around when he went to the two stones at the bottom of the slope.

Near the church was a pair of tourists in matching caps with 'Moose Club' written on them. They were jotting down what the gravestones said in a big pad, and taking pictures of them. Ronnie decided that when he died he'd be cremated, and the ashes would go secretly for medical research. It would be a great mystery what had happened to him.

Things were shaping up just now, anyway. Ronnie had been into parts of the town he had never visited before, and seen things he had never seen. In the interests of business he had taken some of the most valuable-looking things from the 'Misc' bag, stuffed them in his pockets, and gone to Leith Docks.

Most of the people he talked to were small game to someone

like him, but he was a bit frightened all the same. He had the gun in his pocket as well, and he made sure that the people he met saw everything he had on him. They were generally pretty respectful when they saw the gun, though one man called the police and he had to run for it.

Nobody knew who he was. As the day went on he heard rumours and gossip about a place where a man in business for himself could meet others in the trade, compare methods and figures, share experience, make contacts. It sounded like the Small Business Club that Stinker Todd was always on about.

Ronnie's pockets were lighter by the evening, but he was getting places. At last, just as the sun was setting and he was ready to head for home, a greasy wee guy in an antique shop gave him the phone number he wanted. It cost him a diamond ring, but he was sure it was a good investment.

Back at the flat he used his spit-new avocado-green trimphone. The call was better than he could have imagined. He and Will had a bus to do the next morning, and they would carry on as normal. A basic rule of an expanding business was to keep up a good profitable base. Then while Will was out with his bit, Ronnie would be diversifying.

He made for the familiar two gravestones. The cemetery was a lot quieter, but his mood hadn't improved. He sat down with his back against one of the stones and lit a cigarette, hanging his arm over the back of the stone.

'What would ye say if I told you yer son was famous?' he said, staring at the sky. It was getting cloudier towards dusk, and the sky was turning pink. 'Really famous,' Ronnie said. 'Like a hero. Ye didnae ken that, did ye?' He blew a big smoke ring, and then a small one through it. Not many people could do that outdoors. 'I get things done.' He looked down at the ground beneath him. 'I dinnae just lie around all day.'

Ronnie paused, and then flicked his cigarette away, though it was only half-smoked. The grass around the stones was uncut and ragged, and he tugged at the longer blades and threw them in the direction of the cigarette, which was still smoking a few feet away.

'I'm a disadvantaged child, ye know,' he said. 'I've got tae do things on ma own. I havnae got the security of the family unit tae back me up.' There was no good reason why he should be feeling sad. He stood up and kicked at the ground before walking off. 'Judges are lenient on people like me, ye know,' he said.

— 12 —

The solid, middle-aged telex machine had something disquieting about it. It had sat dormant in the corner of the office for countless years, allegedly for use when vital written orders had to be sent at speed. Baird had no idea how it worked, though he knew its aggravating mechanical rattle from the engineer's yearly tests. Its sudden awakening of its own accord was one of the most painful developments in the Highland hold-up case.

Why the Scottish Secretary felt compelled to commit his dirty work to telex was beyond fathoming. Baird had had his share of political interference in a thirty-year career, from discreet letters and telephone calls to whispered words in the corridor, but never, ever, in the form of a telex. Until now.

Word was there were cabinet reshuffles in the pipeline, and the Secretary was getting jumpy. As the weeks went by and the media flap about the bandits grew, the humm, burr and grinding as the telex machine burst into life in the corner became infuriatingly familiar.

It was fine entertainment for the juniors, who had taken to addressing the machine as Henry. Even Bender, who was unaware of its significance, seemed to approve of mechanical activity in the corner of the room.

But off-the-record interference of any kind was offensive to Baird, and the telexes added insult to the injury. He believed the Secretary's typist to be a drunkard or worse, for the messages that unfurled from the innards of the machine often appeared to be in some kind of code which required translation.

Baird stifled a yawn. This wasn't the first time he had found himself on the line to the Secretary's secretary, trying to discover what it was he was supposed to be doing. It was usual to be kept hanging on the telephone for some time, and Baird scanned through *Northern Fly-tying Hints* as he waited. He and Harley had been up till three a.m. the previous night trying to schedule some sort of decent patrol-car cover for the B-roads.

All the other occupants of the room were also on the telephone, except for Harley, who looked as if he was asleep. Beside him, Dunn was talking to one of the bus companies.

'The analysis we have gives a sort o' mixture,' Baird could hear him saying. Dunn pulled a sheet of paper out of the mess on his desk and scanned it.

'Let's see, Hydrotoxalic Acid, Sodium Tripilidide, skin irritants, seasoning –' he paused – 'Aye, seasoning, like for food, spices and stuff.'

Dunn laughed, unaware that Baird was watching him. He doodled a man with two heads on the analysis-sheet as he talked.

'Aye I know,' he said. 'Somebody said a hot bath might help.'

The assistant-secretary to the Secretary came on the line. Yes, he said, the message which Baird had received was the message the Secretary had sent him. He was not familiar with the error Baird was describing in the third line of the second paragraph.

Baird looked at the telex on his desk. 'Maybe the machine's gone wrong,' he said. The assistant-secretary thought that was unlikely, and Baird cut him short. He was a patient man, but enough was enough.

'Yes, well "grunties" is what it says,' he said. He spoke with great restraint. The assistant-secretary was silent.

'Do you suppose the Secretary means guarantees?' Baird said. The assistant-secretary supposed so. 'Well we're in no position to give guarantees of that kind. If they will persist in carrying cash and valuables with them for a bus-trip, what does the Secretary expect?'

The assistant-secretary whined, and Baird could feel his manners deserting him. 'Well maybe they are as stupid as they look,' he said, 'and you can tell that to the Secretary.' The assistant-secretary was silent again, and Baird put the phone down.

He turned the page on *Northern Fly-tying Hints*. This sort of top-level meddling put his nose out of joint, but when it was combined with the mysteries of technology, it was too much. He was beginning the chapter on 'The Insect World' when he became aware of Bender's voice.

'I'm trying to tell you I can't make it to court,' the American was saying. 'Well pay her whatever she wants.'

Baird looked up with interest. Bender was bent over his cordless phone behind his desk, facing the wall as he talked. Suddenly he gave out a loud exclamation.

'That's twice my annual salary!' Baird buried his nose in the book and listened as the American went on in a near-whisper. 'Am I paying for this call? They can't subpoena me, I'm on government business . . . no, it's not a holiday anymore, I can't say how long . . . Visiting rights? We don't have any children.'

Bender's voice had been getting louder again as he talked, and now he shouted with sufficient volume to produce a hush in the main office next door. 'Ben, I love that dog!'

Baird looked up. Dunn was staring at Bender, his mouth hanging open. He nudged Harley with his elbow, but Harley didn't move. Bender glanced quickly around the room and finished his call in a whisper.

'She doesn't even like it. Look I'll try to get back as soon as possible. Call me.'

He clipped the cordless telephone on to his belt and strolled casually across the room. Baird watched as the American perched his fat arse on the edge of Baird's desk, and made himself comfortable.

Nobody sat on Baird's desk. It wasn't a rule, or something anyone said, it was just a way of doing things. Baird smiled benevolently at the trespasser.

Bender said, 'I guess you're pleased with the way this operation is going.' He smiled back at Baird.

Baird took off his glasses, rubbed his eyes and looked at the American. The rash on his flabby cheek was visibly worse, an orange and red crusty patch which looked as if it might be painful. Baird said, 'Have you some sort of complaint to make, Mr Bender?' He realised Dunn was watching from the other side of the room, though Harley was still cradling his head in his arm.

Bender kept his fixed smile. 'See,' he said, 'the way I see it, an outfit like mine could clear this sort of trouble up in a couple of days.'

He carefully straightened some of the papers on Baird's desk and went on, looking directly at Baird.

'Seems to me the English Government might see it that way, too.'

Baird never lost his temper. It got frayed, from time to time, but he never lost it. But it took him every grain of his self-control to keep him sitting as he was. He looked up at Bender questioningly, and then the phone rang.

It was Harley's phone, the blue one, and Harley picked it up without raising his head. 'Operation Bandit,' he said.

They watched him as his bleary eyes slowly opened. They all knew what the blue phone meant. 'Yes,' he said. 'Yes . . . yes . . . aye, aye.' A grin spread across his face, and he covered the mouthpiece of the phone to shout across the room. 'Number Eight. You won't believe this one.'

Dunn reached for a red flag. Bender eased himself off Baird's desk and strolled back to his own, talking to no one in particular. 'Where can I get me a good car around here?' he said.

Will topped up Margot's wine glass and set the bottle down; the light from the single candle flickered in Margot's face as she ate. She looked as if she was in a film.

'You know,' Will said, 'the sunsets seem to be getting nicer every night.'

Margot smiled. He knew she liked sunsets. Only out of the corner of his eye did he see Isla's hand stretch towards the candle and snuff it out with a forkful of steak and kidney pie.

'That's taking my oxygen,' Isla said.

Will couldn't believe it. He watched the last strands of smoke rising from a smear of gravy. 'It took me days to find that candle,' he said.

Isla looked at him as if he was mad. 'It was taking all my oxygen,' she said loudly.

Father picked up the candle carefully and studied it in the light from the sitting-room door. 'You've put steak and kidney pie all over the end,' he said.

Margot was covering up a smile, and Will wished he understood her better. It hadn't been easy, telling Mother and Father about her, and asking if she could come for a meal.

Mother had got really excited and kept asking him if it was serious, and Father wanted to know where he got the money to court a young lady. Then Isla went around singing a song she made up called 'Love On The Dole'. Those were its only words. She even sang it to her aerobics records.

It had been a strain. He was supposed to meet Margot at the bus station at seven the previous night, but he thought it was at eight and missed her. While he was waiting around not knowing he had missed her, she went to the joke shop for him, and Ronnie wouldn't let her in. Will went home late and phoned all the hospitals in Scotland, and then Margot phoned him and said she hadn't been able to get through for hours.

Why did Ronnie not let her in? He had just done a bus with Ronnie, but he didn't manage to ask him. Ronnie was being strange.

Margot gave him a good-telling-off for getting the time wrong, and said what if she turned up two hours late for the family tea? In the end she forgave him and said she was looking forward to it, but Will was very nervous.

He set the table three hours before tea-time, and sat waiting on the balcony. Margot arrived ten minutes early. It had started all right, but nobody had very much to say. Soon they weren't saying anything at all. Will tried to think of something to say. Father had got his hanky out, and he was wiping the end of the candle.

Isla turned to Margot. She had somehow managed to sit next to her, although Will had already arranged the order with Mother.

'Dae you wear suspenders?' Isla said.

Mother spoke very quickly. 'It must be very interesting courying,' she said.

Margot smiled. 'Oh aye,' she said, 'well the country is lovely, and the tourists can get a bit tiresome, but it has its moments.'

Father had gathered the smeared food from the candle into his hanky, and he folded it up and used the hanky to wipe his nose. He spoke as he was wiping, looking into the hanky. 'It's a good steady job,' he said, 'which is more than can be said for some.'

He was bound to start at some point. Will stared at Father, and so did Mother. Father hesitated when he saw they weren't happy, and then he cheerfully grinned at Margot. 'I bet it has got its moments just now with these young bandits in the hills,' he said. 'Have you ever come across them?'

Margot started to shake her head, and suddenly Will thought of something to say. He was getting quite excited.

'Aye,' he said, 'they're really great, aren't they Dad? Oh aye. Really clever. And brave, and they've got initiative, they've got it where it counts, haven't they?'

He was practically dying of excitement. And Father was nodding his head. 'Aye,' Father said, 'I'd give a week's wages to meet those lads.'

Will nearly exploded. Mother was looking strangely at him, and Isla didn't know what was going on. He jittered about in his seat and grinned at Margot.

She was frowning at him. She put her plate to one side and started speaking to Father. 'What's worrying me is what's going to happen to them,' she said. 'I mean, it can't go on forever, can it?'

She had never said anything like that before. It must be because he was so cheeky to Father. But Will hadn't been doing any harm. It was just a joke. Father looked at Margot as if he was a bit offended.

'Och, they'll never get caught,' Father said. 'They're clever, they've got it where it counts. Do you know what they did with a bus of Germans up at Inverleven?'

Will nodded, grinning again. But Margot looked at him very

seriously and interrupted Father again. It wasn't even polite. 'Mr Bryce,' she said, folding her arms on the table, 'they're attacking our biggest industry. Tourism.' Father looked a bit taken aback. Margot went on. 'There's foreigners with influence and money on these tours. And they're making a joke of our police force. They'll get the chop.'

Isla perked up. 'The electric chair!' she said.

Mother stood. 'Who's for more pie?' she said busily.

Father gave up. He was fiddling with the candle again, holding it in his lap and striking matches. 'I can't get it lit,' he said.

After the meal Will and Margot sat outside on the floor of the balcony with their cups of coffee, and didn't say anything for a long time. The distant noises of the city traffic floated through the night air.

Will was lost. Both his lives seemed to be coming off the rails.

Only that morning he'd done a bus with Ronnie. It had been a weekend tour, no problems, except this time Ronnie decided to have a quick look at the passengers' luggage. The two of them got a pile of cases out of the compartment in the side of the bus, and Ronnie started searching through them. There were some funny things in there, but nothing Ronnie wanted. In the end he gave up and started sulking and Will had quickly to try and put all the stuff back in the cases again. He was no good at folding clothes.

Ronnie was bad-tempered all the time. He hardly said anything at all to Will. They used to talk a lot, especially after they'd done buses, about what the passengers were like, and what they'd got in the haversack. It was always exciting. But this morning the only things he said to Will were 'Hullo' and 'Right' and 'That's enough' and 'The luggage' and 'Hurry up and open it ye big idiot'. All he said to the passengers was, 'Anybody here not know the form?'

Maybe he'd practised doing things properly so much that that was all he could do. Being friendly wasn't part of it. He was probably overworked, and they should take a holiday.

But now Margot was saying they were going to get caught by the police. Will hadn't even thought about the police in weeks. It hadn't been important. Ronnie would never let them get caught. Why was she saying that?

The thing you had to do with people you wanted to understand was pretend that you were them, and then you would know how their minds were working. Will watched Margot. She had a lovely blue summer dress on, that she'd worn specially for the family tea. It was all crinkly out at the bottom, and pulled in with a belt at the waist. She had a very thin waist, though she'd just had a big piece of steak and kidney pie. She was looking out at the lights of the city. Will looked at them too.

He was a courier on the buses, and he lived in a wee flat in Newhaven. The sea air would probably give him asthma. Anyway he had a friend he liked very very much, a girl who went as a wolfman and robbed the buses. And he thought she was going to be caught by the police. Why did he think that? Margot thought that, he didn't think it. Maybe she was going through a phase.

'What are you thinking?' Margot said.

He put down his coffee cup and stood up on the balcony. It was time. He was very embarrassed, but he had practised all after-noon, and he was going to do it. He gazed out at the city as he spoke, so that he didn't have to look at Margot. 'And so,' he said, 'among these rocks he lived.' His mind had gone blank, this was what always happened at school. He was bottom in English. He started again, speaking faster so that he wouldn't have time to forget. 'And so among these rocks he lived through summer's heat and winter snow the eagle he was lord above and Rob was lord below.'

That was it. He had found it in his old *Selected Poems of William Wordsworth* from school when he was looking for something nice to say to Margot.

'I beg your pardon?' He turned. Margot was staring at him. He sat down again, hoping he had done the right thing.

'It's a poem,' he said. 'About Rob Roy.' She didn't say anything. 'Remember?' Will said. 'Rob Roy.'

Margot just picked up her coffee and drank, looking at him over the rim of the mug.

From the outside the club looked like an ordinary pub, a pub that didn't have any signs outside and that had seen better days. Its windows were blacked out.

Ronnie shuffled around for a few minutes on the other side of the road, getting ready to go in. It wasn't the best part of town to be hanging around in at this time of night, but he had got there early. He watched a couple of big guys in leather jackets come round the corner, knock on the door and slip inside. They didn't see him.

A black and white dog came up and started sniffing at Ronnie. It sniffed at his feet, and then his socks and then his legs. Ronnie pushed its head away. He ran twenty yards up the road as quietly as possible, and then ran back down again, and the dog followed him, barking. It thought he was playing. Ronnie didn't want to speak to the dog. He hated dogs. Somebody was going to notice him soon. He walked up the road with the dog at his side. It wagged its tail happily. Soon they came to a tip on a stretch of deserted wasteland at the side of the road. The dog sat and waited while he raked about in the rubbish and finally pulled out a two-foot piece of window-frame. He could hear shouting round the corner of a tenement on the other side of the road. It sounded like a gang coming in their direction. Ronnie waved the wood in front of the dog's eyes, then drew his arm back very slowly and hurled it as far as he could over the wasteland. The dog sat and watched him, panting.

Ronnie bent down so his face was right by the dog's, and pointed in the direction he had thrown. 'Fetch,' he hissed. 'Go on, fetch.' The dog looked at him for a long time and then trotted off. Immediately Ronnie sprinted back down the road to the club, and knocked on the door.

He could hear people talking inside. The door opened slowly, and there was a seven-foot man in a T-shirt standing in the doorway. He looked pissed off. His T-shirt had 'I EAT PUNKS' written on it.

'Whit's your game, sonny?' the man said.

Ronnie tried to smile. 'Ronnie Wotherspoon,' he said. He heard a dog barking. He was going to run for it when a fat man hurried up behind the bouncer, smiling at Ronnie.

'It's all right Tam, he's with me,' the fat man said. It was Mr Pyle. The bouncer looked surprised, but he stood aside to let Ronnie in, and Mr Pyle took Ronnie's arm. Glancing back, Ronnie saw the dog appear at the doorway with a shoe in its mouth, looking up at him. The bouncer swore at it and slammed the door.

The club was very smoky, and very crowded. Ronnie blinked, trying to adjust to the dim lighting. It was darker than the street outside.

People were sitting talking and drinking at tables, and a lot of them were crammed up round the bar. Several men stared at Ronnie. There were no women in the club. Ronnie tried not to stare back.

Mr Pyle led Ronnie towards the bar, and as he forced his way through to the counter he shouted to the general crowd: 'Lads, I've got here the seventeenth most wanted man in Scotland.'

Most of the men turned round to see who he meant, and Ronnie couldn't help flinching. He had thought he was higher up on the list than that. Then he heard someone shout 'Welcome tae the club son', and a few men waved and smiled at him, and one wee guy with very thick glasses came up and shook Ronnie's hand, staring at him with enormous eyes.

Mr Pyle asked Ronnie what he wanted, and he ordered a double brandy. Then they pushed through to a table in the corner, and sat down. Ronnie could see a few of the men at the other tables watching him out of the corner of their eyes, and he concentrated on his drink, listening to Mr Pyle.

Mr Pyle was fat and English with long bits of yellow hair at the back of his head. He wore one of those smart jungle suits, and he talked a lot. Even on the telephone he had talked and talked, so that Ronnie's telephone call went on for about an hour. It was the only call he had ever made on his new phone. 'And what about your partner?' Mr Pyle had said. 'Will he be coming too?' Ronnie said no, his assistant didn't take an interest in the business side of things, and when Mr Pyle asked him again in the club he said no, it was just a kid he used to help him out sometimes.

Mr Pyle talked on. He was very interested in Ronnie's career. He finished his beer almost as soon as he sat down and went for another round. Ronnie said, 'Em, I've already got a drink, Mr Pyle.'

'Just call me Pyle,' he said to Ronnie. 'Now listen,' he went on as he banged the glasses down on the table, 'transportation. Think cargo –' he tapped his finger on his beermat – 'passengers –' he tapped again – 'people.' He tapped again, and looked pleased.

Ronnie nodded. He didn't like this club. He could see men still watching him and talking, and he held tightly on to the puffer in his pocket.

'Think class,' Pyle said. 'The right class of people. Where are they going to be?' Ronnie thought. In Morningside, maybe. 'In buses?' Pyle said, and he shook his head. Ronnie shook his head too, and drained his second glass of brandy. 'Not really,' Pyle said. 'Planes?' Ronnie nodded wisely. 'Too much competition,' Pyle said, standing up and collecting the glasses. 'Think cars.' He thumped on the table with the glasses. 'Limousines.' He thumped again. 'Cars.'

While Pyle was at the bar, Ronnie tried to get his bearings. This wasn't how he'd imagined it. His head was a bit fuzzy, but he could see a man with a beard staring at him from the other end of the bar. The man grinned when he saw Ronnie looking at him. He had no front teeth. Ronnie looked away quickly.

Pyle dumped two glasses down on the table and sat down heavily, spilling some of the drinks. He looked seriously at Ronnie.

'Did you ever think of going for private cars?' he said. Ronnie hesitated, and Pyle made a face. The man with no front teeth was standing beside Ronnie, grinning.

94

'Shake pal,' the man said, holding out his hand. Ronnie shook. The man said, 'Oh, I loved what you did tae that Yankee bastard.' He had a Glasgow accent. He pulled a chair over and sat down next to Ronnie.

Ronnie nodded for a while at everybody, and then he realised Pyle was still waiting for him to answer. 'Well, there was a time –' he said, but the Glasgow man interrupted him, slapping his shoulder.

'You just abolished him. That was great.'

Pyle didn't look impressed. 'Hullo Nigel,' he said.

Nigel was still grinning at Ronnie. 'I've got the pictures from the paper at home,' he said. He liked Ronnie. Ronnie smiled at him.

Pyle took a long drink and went on talking, hitting the table as he spoke, and speaking louder to get Ronnie's attention. 'Think potential. We're co-operative here, we help each other. People in cars. Kidnapping, blackmail, hijacking, extortion. We've got contacts. Get yourself a suntan. See the world.'

Nigel leaned aggressively across the table. 'Seen it,' he said.

Ronnie looked at Pyle, and looked at Nigel. 'Aye,' he said. He was feeling generally odd.

At the home he had tried glue-sniffing with the other kids, but it made him feel the same as if he ran round in very tight circles until he fell over, and that was cheaper.

He'd never really had much to drink, he couldn't afford it. Since the business had taken off he was getting a bit of a taste for five-star brandy, but he still wasn't used to more than five or six in a night. The doubles were confusing him, and he tried to think how he could leave without upsetting anyone.

After Pyle brought him his fifth double he stopped drinking them. Pyle was talking on and on, and slowly sinking lower in his seat, and spilling more of his drink every time he brought it back from the bar. Ronnie didn't understand what he was talking about, but it was something to do with Ronnie doing things for Pyle, and he didn't like the idea. Ronnie was his own man. He'd proved it. He didn't like Pyle either. The man was a drunk.

Eventually Pyle stood up, wavering on his feet. Nigel scowled at him. 'Well Lonnie, thing it over,' Pyle said, patting Ronnie on the shoulder, and stumbled out the door.

The dog had gone when Ronnie and Nigel left the club.

Ronnie was still feeling fuzzy, and Nigel said he was going in the same direction as Ronnie for his bus. Nigel had been sitting quietly next to Ronnie in the club, making faces at Pyle. He was all right.

'Aye, he's a namby-pamby bastard that Pyle,' Nigel said as they walked up the narrow street.

Ronnie looked up at him. Nigel was built like a block of flats. He had a big brown leather coat that reached nearly to his ankles, greasy hair, and a battered face. He had been around.

'Aye,' Ronnie said. 'Well ye know – aye. Yes he is, really, namby-pamby.'

He could hear shouting round the corner, and four skinheads bolted out of a close into the street. Two of them were carrying sticks. Ronnie grabbed Nigel's arm without thinking, looking for a place to hide, but the skinheads took one look at Nigel and walked off in the other direction. Nigel hadn't even noticed.

'It was different in the old days,' he said. 'See me? I've got a gun now. Guns are for lassies. Naebody seems tae put the boot in anymair.'

'No,' Ronnie said. 'No, I ken what ye mean. They just don't.'

Nigel stopped, digging in his coat pockets, and brought out a packet of cigarettes. He gave one to Ronnie, took one himself, and lit them. They strolled on, and Ronnie tried walking like Nigel, his feet pointing outwards, his back straight and his chest stuck out. It felt good. When he was younger he would have run through this part of town without pausing for breath.

'I mean,' Nigel said, 'all that potential and co-operation an' pish like that –' he turned to Ronnie – 'gets on ma tits.'

'Aye,' Ronnie said.

'Ye dinnae want tae bother wi' that shite,' Nigel said.

'No,' Ronnie said. He really meant it.

Nigel stopped again, studying Ronnie. 'D'ye need them glasses?' he said. Ronnie put a hand up to his glasses, still looking at Nigel, and took them off. No, he thought, probably not. 'Ye dinnae want glass goin' in your eye when some bastard stands on your face,' Nigel was saying. He waved a hand in front of Ronnie's face. 'See this?' he said. Ronnie screwed up his eyes and strained to see, but in the end he had to put the glasses back on. Nigel was pointing at his own eyes. 'Contact lenses,' he said. 'Changed ma life.' They walked on.

A drunk was staggering around on the pavement in front of them, going nowhere in particular, and Nigel put his hand out and swept the man out of the way without even looking at him. Nigel had style.

'Soft lenses too, the expensive ones,' he said. 'See ma optician kens his arse frae his elbow.' Nigel turned to look at Ronnie, grinning with his gums.

'That's what I like about you,' he said. 'Ye get on your motorbike, ye go out there an' ye say what ye want. An' if ye dinnae get it –' Nigel's grin got bigger – 'mutilation.'

Ronnie grinned back. Everything was still fuzzy, but he knew what this was all about.

'Aye,' he said. It was embarrassing how well he and Nigel understood each other. 'Mutilation.'

For about three years, Ronnie had hated Don Robertson more than anyone else in the world. Don Robertson was the leader of the gang, Young Mental Belside, and he stayed at the home. He was bigger than anyone else their age, and he didn't like Ronnie. Ronnie wanted to be in the gang.

Don would hit him on the back of the head until Ronnie lost his temper, just trying to get Ronnie to hit him back so that Don could kill him. All the time he laughed away at Ronnie like it was the best joke in the world. Once Ronnie did lose his temper, but he wasn't very good at fighting, and the gang hung him out the window and melted his glasses.

One day Don Robertson came up to him and said, 'Okay Ronnie, you're old enough now, why don't you come out with us tonight.' It was the first time he hadn't called him Spoonhead. Don sat talking to him for a while and told him all the things they were going to do after dark. They were coming down hard on bus shelters, he said.

Ronnie could hardly believe it. He got all his best bad clothes out and went to meet the gang after tea. They didn't talk much, but they were a good bunch of lads. They went round to the bus shelter in Belside Terrace, and tore the hell out of it. Charlie Grant lent Ronnie his stick, and Ronnie did two windows himself. Two of them stood on the roof and brought that down, and then they got the paint out – two pots nicked from the ironmonger's – to write their name. Except they threw the paint over Ronnie and ran off.

Ronnie had paint in his eyes, but he heard Don Robertson laughing. He ran towards the home, and then found he was leaving a trail of footprints from the bus shelter. He had to run in circles and hide in someone's garden until he dried. Then he climbed into the home after lights out. He never spoke to Don Robertson again.

Nigel had been in gangs too, but men's gangs, not boys'. He had been a hard man in Glasgow, and he'd seen it all. For a long time he'd been in a gang with Harry Niven, who was the real top hard man. Nigel had been in prison eighteen times since he was ten years old. He knew the form.

Ronnie started taking the bike out to Craigmuir when he wasn't working. Nigel lived in a caravan in the back garden of an old factory, and he liked to see Ronnie. He respected him for what he had done, and he said he was going to show Ronnie the ropes.

The caravan was in a terrible state. Nigel had burned most of the furniture for a barbecue, and he just had an old mattress on the floor inside. The mattress was burned a bit too. There was no proper light inside because Nigel had painted the windows over with white paint to reflect atomic glare. The only thing in the world that scared him was nuclear war. He had magazines about how many missiles the Americans and the Russians had and what cruise missiles did and how many people would be killed if someone dropped a bomb on Liverpool.

But they sat on the step and Nigel told Ronnie what it was like to be a hard man. A lot of people thought it was all gratuitous violence and stuff, but it was more to do with mental attitude. Status was very important, and knowing you were better than the other man, and not being afraid of anybody. Ronnie didn't mind the clown and the wolfman, that was his business – although it v as time it became strictly business and none of Will's childish antics – but he felt much better about life now. Nigel was character-developing.

He never mentioned Nigel to Will. There was no reason why he should. He went with Nigel into town, and at the Kazan Discount Stores he tried on a leather coat. It was just like Nigel's except black, and Nigel looked Ronnie up and down as he put it on in front of the mirror. He tried the collar up and down, buttoned and open, hands in and out of pockets. Nigel nodded, and Ronnie paid for it. It was expensive, but it had style.

Nigel decided Ronnie was ready to try the gun. It was a shotgun with the front sawn off, and Nigel had a special pocket in his coat so he could carry it without anyone seeing. They set up a bottle on a half-demolished wall at the back of the empty factory, and Nigel put the gun in Ronnie's hand. It was heavy. Ronnie lifted it up to point in the direction of the bottle, and squeezed the trigger. His hands were shaking.

The bang was louder than anything he'd heard in his life, and suddenly Ronnie was lying on his back. He thought he'd shot himself, but then he heard Nigel saying good shot. When he got up again he looked for the bottle, but there was a great big hole in the wall where it had been standing. Nigel was pretty chuffed.

Sometimes Ronnie would ask Nigel a question, and Nigel wouldn't answer. His head went all wobbly on his neck, and he shut his eyes, and then he would start talking and moaning to himself. Ronnie couldn't get any sense out of him. He told him to wake up and stop it, but Nigel didn't seem to hear him. It could go on like that for hours, and then suddenly Nigel would open his eyes again and answer Ronnie's question as if nothing had happened. It usually wasn't the right answer, but Ronnie was always glad when he woke up.

The thing about a hard man was, he was a man on his own, going his own way. Ronnie started riding the motorbike on his own, which was something he'd never really done since he got it. He would put on his leather coat and his helmet with the mirrored visor and just cruise around the streets at night, not too fast, seeing what was going on. He knew that everybody who saw him would wonder what he was doing, and would respect the stranger in the leather coat.

– 14 –

Nothing was impossible until you'd tried it. Ronnie always used to say that to Will when they were discussing one of Ronnie's ideas.

The more Will thought about things, the more sure he was that it was up to him now to do what was impossible. He'd have to sort out his two lives. But he couldn't imagine Margot and Ronnie being friends. Everybody was behaving so strangely, and the only way Will could think of making things better was to bring it all out into the open, and let it resolve itself once and for all.

Now, whenever he saw Margot they just sat around and did nothing. She didn't want to go out for expeditions and adventures, she wasn't interested. She wanted to be with him, she said. But they hardly ever talked about anything much, except the weather, and the passengers on one of her buses, and Mother's aerobics lessons. It was as if Margot was waiting for something, waiting for Will to come to some decision, or to say something.

Will bought her flowers. He went to the fruit shop and paid two pounds, and the girl in the shop chose them specially herself. He made himself be brave. But Margot said thank you and put them in a vase and nothing changed. Then he nearly asked her to marry him, but just in time she said how people shouldn't get married until they were secure. He didn't know what to do.

Even his warts were behaving strangely. After they had first started and grown on his hand, they had stopped changing and gone hard and crusty. He hadn't had a new wart in weeks. He rubbed at the old ones with the gold brooch, every day, but it didn't make any difference.

Father said Will had been on the dole long enough now, and it was time he started putting his money where his mouth was. Will was certain Father wanted him to go to New Mexico and make his fortune like Carol Paton's big brother.

Then the cat crawled into his bed and wouldn't come out all day. Everybody huddled round very sad and thought it was dying, but when darkness came it peed in the bed and hopped out as fit as a fiddle.

So when he went to the joke shop Will knew he had to do the impossible. He chose a Monday afternoon, when he knew it would be quiet.

After he had said hullo and Ronnie had grunted, Will tried to get on to the important subject in as roundabout a way as he could. It wasn't easy, because Ronnie was worse than ever. He had bought a big black leather coat like they used to wear in the Sixties, and he stamped about behind the counter, snorting. He even looked different, sort of sticking his chest out and waddling like a duck.

Will had thought very carefully about how to make his plan seem like a nice idea. It was going to be a picnic, at the seaside. He and Ronnie used to go down to Portobello when they were at school and go on the funfair, and he knew Ronnie would like that. Ronnie loved the dodgems, he was a good driver, and he was great at the penny falls. He had a way of shaking the machine so that the money came out without setting off the alarm.

They would go on the bus, Will, Margot and Ronnie, and they would take sandwiches to eat on the bus, and then at Portobello they would get candy-floss and toffee apples and discuss things. That was what he said to Ronnie.

But the more words he used, the more fed-up Ronnie's face became, until he was shaking his head from side to side like somebody looking at a really pathetic sight.

'And – candy-floss,' said Will.

Ronnie glared at him.

'Have I not made mysel' clear?' he shouted. 'Women are nothin' but trouble, you should start tae think about that.'

He waved his arm about. 'It's all you think about. Half the bus station probably knows about us because o' you and your women.' Ronnie stopped shouting, and stared about the shop as if he'd just come through a time-warp and had no idea where he was. Will didn't know what to do. Ronnie usually lost his temper about twice a week, and when it happened there was nothing you could do except wait until he got it back again. But everything Will wanted to say to Ronnie these days made him lose his temper.

'I only wanted –' Will said quietly, but Ronnie interrupted him.

'I'm goin' tae leave this place soon,' he said. 'It's no' ma scene. Times are changin', pal, ye've got tae change with them.'

Will had tried, and it was impossible. He looked up at Ronnie. 'I was only trying –' he said, but as he spoke two wee boys stuck their heads in the shop door. Ronnie shouted furiously at them.

'We're closed!'

Tea was terrible. Father was still on about Will's unemployment, and Mother didn't say anything to dampen him down. Isla didn't say anything either, but just sat staring at Will with a little grin on her face as she chewed.

Afterwards he phoned Margot, but she said she was very tired and was just going to bed. It was only eight o'clock. 'Did you have anything to say to me?' she said. She was still waiting for him to do something. 'I hope ye sleep well,' Will said. He didn't tell her about going to see Ronnie.

Mother was washing the dishes and Father was reading the paper in the kitchen, and Will went next door and slumped on the sofa in front of the telly. Isla had disappeared.

It was a news programme about him and Ronnie. Will watched

in a daze as the camera showed the series of spots where they'd done the hold-ups. Maybe the police were going to catch them after all.

The picture cut to the old man with the beard they'd seen in the paper. 'Superintendent James Baird, co-ordinator, Operation Bandit', it said on the screen. He was wearing a deerstalker hat, talking to an interviewer. 'I think it's fair to say, at the moment, that we are optimistic about an early arrest,' he said.

The picture on the screen changed to the photo-booth photograph Ronnie had sent to the telly people. 'Forensic experts are currently studying the picture in the hope it may give them the clue they are looking for,' said the commentator.

'Mind if I join you?'

Will looked up. It was Isla, sitting down on the chair next to the settee. He grunted, and turned back to the screen. They were showing pictures of the bus station, with buses coming and going out of the entrance. Will peered to see if he could see Margot.

Then he looked back at Isla. He had known her for twelve years, and in all that time he had never, ever heard her being polite like that. She smiled at him for a moment and watched the telly. Maybe she felt sorry for him. You could sense when something was wrong with someone in your own family.

The picture on the screen changed to two wee Japanese men in dark suits and ties, talking to an interviewer. Behind them were two wee orange cars with sun-roofs. The commentary went on.

'As the Scottish Liberation Front and the Caledonian National Group both claimed responsibility for the hold-ups, the search for the pirates was joined today by an unusual expedition from the land of the rising sun. The nine-man television crew from Tokyo want to be the first to film the bandits in action, though their arrival has caused some anger among the local media and police.'

Now the sound came on from the interviewer talking to the Japanese men.

'Don't you think your presence might get in the way of any police operations which may be taking place to catch the bandits?' the interviewer said.

One of the men answered him, smiling. 'No, I, ah, we are not here for . . . revenge . . . we only want . . . to . . . and to, ah, film it . . . for our programme,' he said.

Revenge? Will could remember seeing a few Japanese people here and there on the buses, but they had never done anything nasty to any of them. Certainly never puffed any of them. What would they want revenge for? If people felt really bad about things, he was sure they could get their money back to them somehow.

The television report changed to the opening of a cheese factory in Glenrothes. 'The new curd-masher does the job in half the time,' someone said.

'When's the next hold-up,' someone said.

Will looked round. The only other person in the room was Isla, and she was watching the telly. 'What?' he said. She turned, playing with the sleeve of her jumper.

'Oh, I was just wonderin', when ye thought these men might dae the next hold-up, ye know, up North.' She smiled.

It was all right, it would be all right, he just had to stay on top of things and nothing would happen.

'Oh aye,' Will said, shifting about in the seat. 'Hold-up, hold-up.' He looked innocently at Isla. 'What hold-up? There's a lot of funny things goin' on, ye know, ye should read the papers, course I havnae really been followin'.' He sat back, shifting again, but managing to talk quite successfully. There was no expression on Isla's face. 'Hold-up,' Will went on, 'well these things just happen out the blue, don't they, one minute you're just sittin' there quite normally, and the next – aye, yes.' He shrugged. 'Well, who knows, who knows.'

There was silence. Slowly he turned to look at Isla. She gazed blankly at him. 'I do,' she said. 'And you do. And Ronnie Wotherspoon knows.'

Will had read somewhere that when an animal is in the most terrible danger and there is no possible chance of escaping the final deadly blow, a special chemical is released into its blood that paralyses it and stops it from feeling pain. This happened to Will as Isla got up from her seat and switched off the telly. Only his eyes moved, following her over to the curtain in front of the French window to the balcony. He watched as she opened the balcony door, and watched her six girlfriends appear as calmly as if they had just walked in the front door.

They lined up in front of him, roughly in order of height. Will recognised six-year-old Mary Harrison from two flats down, and Lizzie Dundas, who was just a bit younger than Isla, and he'd seen the other faces around. They were all looking at him very seriously.

Isla shut the French window and came round to stand in front of Will. 'We've all got birthdays comin' up ye know,' she said.

Summer was nearly through. The Festival only had another week to run, and soon the leaves would be turning and the autumn winds would whip through the city. The weather had been changeable for a while, and there might not be many sunny days left.

The sky was a wispy grey as Will watched Margot pacing along the concrete foreshore at Newhaven. She was wrapped in her raincoat, and a scarf fluttered at her neck.

It had taken him hours to find Ronnie. He wasn't at the bedsit and he wasn't at the shop, and Will simply didn't know where else to look. For weeks now the only times he could be sure of being able to see Ronnie were when Ronnie was working in the shop. He had no idea where Ronnie went all the time, and he didn't like to ask.

Will ran his hand through his hair. Ronnie hadn't been at the bedsit last night, and Will hadn't slept properly. He kept trying to make plans and sort things out in his mind, but he knew he couldn't do it without Ronnie.

Eventually he came to the shore to see Margot, and got through to Ronnie from the phone box, but Ronnie didn't seem to understand what had happened.

'I made them all promise an oath of secrecy,' Will said into the phone. 'I said –' he hesitated. He knew what Ronnie would think. 'I said they could be honorary members of the gang if they could prove they could keep a secret. And some more jewellery.'

Luckily he'd had some stuff in his jacket pockets which hadn't fitted into the haversack on the last bus, and he'd been able to give them one piece each. He didn't give them his brooch, though.

'They want identity cards sayin' they're members,' Will said. 'Oh God.'

Ronnie's business voice came down the line.

'Keep the heid, will ye, pal? Are you tryin' tae tell me you're scared o' a bunch o' wee lassies?'

What could Will say? He watched Margot walking along the shore, her back to him now. He hadn't told her what had happened, but she knew something was wrong, and she was very nice to him. She didn't seem surprised something bad had happened, and Will could feel she was expecting something to come out of it, in the end. But she wasn't pressing him. He watched as she bent down to look at something in a puddle. She had a brilliant bum.

'You're in the big time now, ye know,' Ronnie was saying. 'Kids can get damaged messin' wi' people like us. You know, mutilation, sort of.'

Will could hear a horrible laugh in the background. This time he had to ask.

'Who is it ye've got there with ye?'

Ronnie didn't answer. He went on at Will about how Will could take care of the problems with the girls, there was nothing to get over-excited about, and anyway it was his sister. And did Will realise they were going on a job tomorrow?

Will thought. Had he over-reacted about the whole thing? He looked at Margot walking slowly up the shore, staring out to sea. She pushed a strand of hair away from her face. She was beautiful.

He could probably keep the girls happy for a while, as long as Isla was getting what she wanted. Like Ronnie said, who would believe them anyway? One more job wouldn't make any difference. But he'd have to discuss it more when he saw Ronnie. They ought to be careful or the police would catch them.

'I'll talk to them again,' he said.

Ronnie said he'd see him tomorrow, and the line went dead.

Will looked up. Margot was walking up from the shore. She waved. He waved back, making himself smile.

- 15 -

今、現場の カメラマンが、頑強な 2つの車輪で支えられた いかにも勇壮果敢な 「ハイランド・ヒーロー」の うわさ高い容姿を とらえました。

「自由」、それは、普段、私達が あまりにも何気なく 使っていることばではありますが、ここ バイクの世界では いたる所で、この「自由」が いきづいているのです。*

If it hadn't been for the blasted Japanese, Baird would have had it all sewn up.

It wasn't the sort of calculation he expected to work. Dunn and Harley had come to the conclusion that all the hold-ups took place on either Tuesday mornings, Thursday afternoons or Sundays. There hadn't been a robbery for over a week, and the next Tuesday fell ten days after the last hold-up, so they decided to give it a try. There was nothing else for them to do, and frankly they hadn't much to lose.

There were three possible spots. A remote glen in the Northwestern Highlands which would be crossed by a party of English

---

* 'Freedom – an easy word to use casually – but this is what the motorcycle life is all about.' Quoted by kind permission of the Imperial Motorcycle Corporation, Tokyo, Japan.

pensioners on a week's trip; a Perthshire side-road which a day-excursion of Americans from Edinburgh would be taking towards Callendar for lunch; and a twisting mountain road down towards Lochgoilhead, the route for a day-excursion of mixed tourists from Glasgow. None of them were near the sites of any other hold-ups, and they all seemed equally unlikely.

Late that night they put the names in Baird's deerstalker, and Harley pulled out Lochgoilhead. Dunn told Bender next morning that the target had been forecast by the computer at HQ, which had some poetic truth about it.

They made a chilly dawn start on Tuesday, travelling North in time to set everything up before the morning had properly begun. When they were ready Baird sent Dunn and Harley in one car and two uniformed officers in another to make a quiet search through the area, and the rest of them sat and waited. The Japanese were out there somewhere as well.

There was nothing Baird could do about the Japanese television people. They had two wee orange Japanese cars completely kitted out, with cameras and microphones and stuff sticking out of their sun-roofs and windows, and they were tenacious wee buggers. As long as they stuck to the public roads, Baird had no way of stopping them.

At about the time the Glasgow bus was due, Dunn and Harley spotted two figures standing on the crest of a hill at the top of a steep side-road, watching them. It was the clown and the wolf-man.

Dunn and Harley were shitting themselves. They had no idea how long the bandits had had them under surveillance, or what they were planning. They radioed the other patrol, and the two cars sped up the hilly road as fast as they could go. They could see the clown and the wolfman running to a motorbike and starting up.

It was about this time the Japanese appeared. As Harley described it, they came rattling straight across the side of the hill, dodging boulders and bushes, and aiming their cameras and equipment at the disappearing motorbike on the top. Many of them were hanging out the windows of the little orange cars, waving and shouting, and they skidded on to the tarmac road directly in front of the juniors' car and carried on in pursuit of the motorbike.

It was in this state that the cars careered over the top of the hill and raced headlong down the other side towards Lochgoilhead behind the motorbike. By all accounts Dunn was driving very well, but he couldn't manoeuvre the car past the Japanese. They were swerving all over the place, waving and shouting, and they paid not the slightest attention to his siren and lights, or his many attempts to overtake. While the leading Japanese car was clearly filming the motorbike in front of it, the crew in the car which Dunn and Harley were chasing was filming them, as they cursed and waved the Japanese to pull over.

By the time the procession was a mile outside the village, the cars had gained a lot of ground on the fleeing bandits. Indeed Dunn's report claimed that the leading Japanese car was no more than a hundred yards behind the motorbike. Suddenly Baird and his team heard a distant bang, and Harley's fearful voice came over the radio.

'Come in control, they're firing on us.'

As the Japanese edged closer and closer to the motorbike, the wolfman had turned round and flung something at the cars. It exploded in a shower of sparks, causing the Japanese to swerve, but not to stop. The wolfman tried again, and there was another explosion, but the second missile also went off harmlessly in the air.

In the village the second bang was louder, and Baird told his marksmen to be ready. Everybody was still, listening as the noise of a motorbike engine grew from a buzz to a clatter. Suddenly it was visible, speeding round the corner and down towards the village, with four cars close behind.

It was quite possible they would crash straight into the barricade, and Baird's men got ready to dive to the side. They watched through the barriers and windows of parked vehicles as the bike came hurtling towards them, skidded to one side, and shot round the back of the petrol station. The four cars arrived at the barricade all at once, slamming to a stop just in front of the barriers in a sort of sandwich.

A great plume of smoke rose from the ground in front of them, and there was a loud hissing noise. The wolfman had thrown something down as he passed. Baird shouted 'Cover!' and every-body ducked.

As he squinted apprehensively over the roof of a land-rover, Baird was horrified to see Dunn getting out of his car, and walking very slowly towards the smoking object. Dunn's eyes were nar-rowed, and his jaw was set in the closest he could get to grim determination.

'I'll handle this,' he said.

Almost instantly the object gave off a terrifying hiss and burst into a genteel fountain of different-coloured sparklers.

Baird's team appeared one by one from behind their cover, and Bender fixed Baird with a long piggy stare. It had been a bad week for the American. The Chief had already nixed the idea of a foreign officer carrying a gun, and he had been very sore about that. But he didn't say a word to Baird for the rest of the afternoon. It was the one bright note in a very bleak day.

By the time the team was mobile again there was no sign of the bandits anywhere. Baird relieved some of his feelings on the Japanese and packed them off to Edinburgh under guard. The Secretary had the charges dropped after two days in the interests of international trade. Only much later did Baird learn that they had been there on behalf of the manufacturers of the wretched motorbike, making a film advertisement.

It was seen by seven and a half million Japanese viewers, the press office told him. It included studio footage of the Japanese journalists inspecting a spot-lit, well-polished model of the motorbike the clown and wolfman were using. In the studio with them the advertisers had large cardboard cut-outs of the bandits, waving at the cameras. The centrepiece of the advertisement was a four-minute film of the clown and the wolfman escaping from the police on the road to Lochgoilhead.

Baird set up a debriefing centre in the village hall, and they tried to get what they could out of the locals. By that time the Scottish press had turned up, and the place was a circus. All two classes of the local school were let out early so they could come and see what was happening, and Baird couldn't get rid of a piper who said he had to practice for the Highland Games.

Some fifty people had seen something of the clown, and the wolfman, by hanging out of their windows or watching from the streets or the fields. The action had happened around noon, and many of them had rushed out of the pub. They took some settling down, but Baird wanted something from all of them. There was nothing else to do.

He sat late in the office, reading over the statements. He was more tired than he'd been in a long time, and he had a stotter of a headache. He'd said he wanted every syllable the witnesses said, and Dunn and Harley had taken him at his word. Baird could feel the noose tightening around his neck with each report he read.

Jimmy Guthrie, 14 Shore Street, age 11, occupation – scholar: 'I was up on the hills I wasn't skiving school I was just going for a breath of fresh air, when I saw them. They were coming down the road from the Rest And Be Thankful, they were going a hundred miles an hour – a hundred and fifty . . .

'. . . then all the cars were coming down right behind them, all over the place, and suddenly Pchhhhhhh! (Witness waves arms about.)

'It was great.'

Mrs Mary Scott, 2 Churchside Road, age 47, occupation – housewife: 'I've nothing against foreigners, my husband's a Perthshire man, but all these police had come from Inverness or somewhere . . .

'They'd been building that barricade all morning. I said to them, I said, you think that'll stop them?'

Ewan Campbell, 9a Dundas Street, age 25, occupation – farm labourer: 'Yes it was a Japanese machine, they can go along a fair nip (witness laughs) . . .

'. . . you see a motorbike's a grand thing to have in these parts, do you know what I mean? I had a bike myself you know, it was a Kawasaki, very good on petrol . . .'

David Smaill, 22 Churchside Road, age 63, occupation – unemployed: '. . . and then very slowly, the bike started to take off. It rose into the air, flew a great circle over the village, and then it disappeared up into a cloud.

'. . . nothing serious, no no, not at all, it was only lunchtime.

'. . . well I had had a couple of drams.'

Ronnie and Will stood on the hillside in the setting sun, watching the lights of the police cars flashing in the distant fields. They were getting further away.

Ronnie lit a cigarette and took a deep puff. Will had nearly done it this time, he really had.

It had been a perfectly straightforward bus, nothing to worry about, and they had had the bad luck to run into a patrol car. They'd seen the police before they were spotted, watching from the top of the hill for the bus, and they managed to get a good start heading down towards Lochgoilhead.

That policeman must have got on to his radio like greased lightning, because suddenly there were police cars everywhere, and camera cars, coming up behind them.

And Will had panicked. The Roadburner was a fine bike, it had carried them safely through a lot of trouble, but nobody could expect it to go faster than a car. Will had just lost his head, bashing on Ronnie's back, going 'Faster! Faster!' all the time. Then he shouted, 'I thought ye said you'd tuned the engine up.'

They were shooting down the valley road, and the cars were getting closer all the time. Ronnie *had* tuned the engine up. He'd cleaned the spark plugs and topped up the oil and checked the water and everything, only the night before. Will had no right to say that.

'Are you just goin' tae sit there gabbin'?' Ronnie shouted back.

'D'ye want me tae get aff an' push?' said Will. Cheeky git.

Ronnie tried to turn round and give him a look, but they were on a steep bend and he nearly lost control of the bike. He could feel Will fumbling with the bag behind him, and heard him say 'Oh aye'.

The cars were getting bigger in Ronnie's mirror. Little people were leaning out of all the windows of the camera cars, waving their arms and shouting at him.

'Will ye slow down?' Will shouted. 'I cannae get it lit.'

It was unbelievable. Ronnie took the cigarette out of his mouth and passed it back without a word. There was a sudden hiss and then a bang, and he could see the explosion in his mirror. It was away up in the air. Will did another one, but it was no better.

They came round the corner on to the road through the village with the cars still right behind them, and Ronnie saw it. A barricade. A solid great barricade, right across the road, with cars and bits of stripey wood and loads of policemen. The ones in the car must have fixed it up with the local police on their radio as soon as they spotted them.

There was nowhere else to go. They were doing sixty, straight for it, and Ronnie wasn't going to slow down. He could see people running to the sides behind the barricade. They'd remember him. He closed his eyes, and then he heard Will shouting.

'Ronnie, the petrol station! The petrol station! Ronnie!'

He opened his eyes. Sure enough, there seemed to be a path behind the petrol station at the side of the road. They had nearly passed it now, about thirty feet from the barricade. He slammed the brakes on and skidded hard round on one side, and then hammered the bike straight back through the petrol station.

It was about thirty seconds before he realised Will was still there behind him. They sped up the little path on to a steep village road, back down on to the far side of the village, and out into the hills again. In a sheltered spot under a clump of trees about fifteen miles out they settled down to wait until dark before travelling back to Edinburgh.

Will had some jam sandwiches in his bag, and they ate those without talking. Ronnie thought. It was no good, he couldn't go on operating with Will. He couldn't rely on him in an emergency. It was time he expanded his personnel.

Even now Will looked pretty scared. He sat on the heather, rubbing at the warts on his hand, and turned to Ronnie. 'That was nearly it, that time, ye know,' he said.

Ronnie watched the flashing lights in the distance. He couldn't help feeling angry. 'Ye just used the mini-rockets, didn't you?' he said. Will shook his head.

'That Star-blaster thing would have blown them up, Ronnie,' he said.

What an attitude. The fireworks had just come into the shop at the beginning of the week, new stock for November. It had given Ronnie one of his best ideas, though Will kept saying they should only use them for emergencies. Well if that wasn't an emergency, what was? Ronnie stubbed out his cigarette and got the bike ready to go.

As they were coming down through Fife towards the Firth of Forth, Will lit the Star-blaster and shot it into the sky. It soared very high, and burst in a huge cloud of red and green lights, way across the county. Ronnie watched angrily as the flares dwindled and died in the darkness.

– 16 –

There were two sorts of people in the world: worriers and non-worriers. Worriers had bags under their eyes and grey hair falling out and upset stomachs. Nobody liked worriers.

Non-worriers had big smiles with white teeth and lots of friends. Fat people were non-worriers. Will checked himself in the bathroom, and made a plan.

At tea he asked Mother for an extra helping. It was like Oliver in the film. Father stared at him and Isla and Mother looked worried. There weren't any extra helpings. He made himself four slices of toast with butter and stuffed them down. He wasn't hungry, but he was determined, and he knew Margot would be pleased because he had decided something. He ate an old apple that was on the sideboard, and some soft biscuits from the tin. Then he had a cup of tea and went to bed.

Next morning he had an upset stomach. He didn't want to go too far from the house, but he knew that the secret of life was being happy within yourself, and not worrying about what was going on around you. He stayed in bed all morning, not knowing what to do, and then he got up and went into town.

It was a busy, sunny day, and he wandered around the shops bumping into tourists. He smiled at them all. One or two people smiled back, but a woman in Goldstein's department store looked at him and hurried her two wee children in the other direction. After a while he found himself going towards the joke shop, and decided that was a good plan.

He wouldn't ask Ronnie any questions, or touch anything in the shop, or interrupt while Ronnie was talking, or do anything that might spoil the day. He would help with anything if Ronnie asked him too, and if Ronnie didn't want him to be there, he would smile a jolly smile and go away again.

But when Will got to the joke shop there was a sign on the door saying 'Closed'. It was locked. The clock in the street said twenty past three, and Will couldn't think what had happened. Ronnie and he must have picked up the same bug in the Highlands, and Ronnie was probably lying ill in bed with a shared toilet.

Will walked quickly towards the bedsit. He could get the keys from Ronnie and open the shop, and they could still make a profit today. If he was fast he could get back by the time the kids came out of school, and everything would look normal when Mr Hardwick inspected the books on Friday.

Will ran through the main door and up the corridor to Ronnie's bedsit, and rapped out the code knock on Ronnie's door. Bang-bangbang – bang – bang – bangbang. No answer. He could hear laughing, and somebody singing.

'Ronnie?' he said.

The door opened a bit, and Ronnie stuck his head round it. He was dressed, but he didn't look very well. He was swaying.

'What is it?' Ronnie said.

'You're not at the shop.'

Ronnie looked at him. Will could smell something like a mixture of old wine, prawn cocktails and the cat. It wasn't very nice.

'I'm a bit busy just now,' Ronnie said.

Will tried to look round the door. 'What's that smell?' he said. There was a loud shout from inside the room.

'Come on Rammer, ye tryin' tae hide one o' your women?'

Will just stood. Ronnie smiled a half-smile at him. The door opened wider and another head came round it beside Ronnie's. It was a big head with greasy hair and a beard, that looked as if it had been battered in at the front. It smiled at Will. It didn't have any front teeth.

'Hiya big boy,' it said, 'come an' join the pairty.'

The funny smell was stronger. A hand came round the door and pulled Will into the room.

Baird was just getting ready to leave the office when Bender turned up.

It was past ten, and Baird was set on getting a good night's sleep. All he could do after the Lochgoilhead fiasco was make a good show of tightening security cover and officially request more resources, and he'd spent the day on it. If they could get a couple of helicopter patrols up in the hills every day he would feel a lot happier, but the chances of anyone coming up with the money for that were slim. It couldn't be long now, but it still looked like a waiting game.

The press were having their usual merry dance about Lochgoilhead, and there was very little he could do about that, too. The bandits had 'slipped through the police dragnet' according to the television reports. The entire Scottish police force didn't have the resources to cover all the roads out of the main towns, and spot checks on Highland roads were just as hopeless. Why should the bandits travel on roads? On a motorbike, a couple of kids could have the run of the country.

He hadn't even been able to save his own face by blaming the bloody Japs because of political shenanigans. The only villainous face that was emerging from this chamber of horrors was James Baird's.

He grabbed his jacket and hat and his new copy of *Trout' Mackenzie Remembers* from the locker, and was just switching off his desk light when Bender appeared in the doorway.

He hadn't spoken to the American since Lochgoilhead, and he could imagine what he would have to say now. He turned the light on again and kept his finger hopefully on the switch.

Bender slid his arse on to the edge of Baird's desk. His face was quite expressionless.

'I thought the barricade was meant to stop the bandits, not the Goddamn squad cars,' he said.

Baird sighed, switched off the light and buttoned up his jacket. He'd had enough of international hospitality. A loud wailing filled the room, and Bender clutched at his belt. His phone was ringing. 'I'm busy,' he barked into it, his eyes still on Baird. 'That's a lie!'

Baird watched with interest as the American hunched over the phone and took a few paces towards the other side of the room. So quietly was he speaking that his words almost disappeared in an indistinct mumble. Baird strained his ears.

'Now listen Ben,' Bender whispered, 'whatever she says, man to man, you've got to believe me, that has never been a problem of mine.' He snorted and stood up straight, waving his free hand, and Baird had no trouble hearing him now. 'I said I do not have that problem. Okay. Did you see the dog? Was his nose cold? Okay. Bye.'

Bender snapped the phone back on his belt. Baird didn't bother to hide his amusement as the American came back towards him, his piggy eyes sparking.

'This whole operation ought to have a kick in the Goddamn butt,' Bender said. Baird picked up his book and hat with a smile.

'I'll bear your comments in mind, Mr Bender,' he said.

Bender touched his arm to stop him, looking into his eyes. Baird gaped. People maybe stuck their arses on the edge of his desk, but nobody touched him. Nobody.

'You'll do more than that, Mr Baird,' the American said. He reached into his jacket and brought out a sheet of paper.

'Special powers from your Mr Secretary. This is my case now. I don't think I'll be needing you any more.' Bender smiled and went to his desk, where he made himself comfortable.

Baird scanned the paper. A telex. It was a telex, from the Secretary, out of that Godforsaken machine in the corner. 'Designated authority,' it said.

He read it twice. It wasn't official, it wasn't on record, Baird had no right of appeal or protest. There was nothing he could do. The American had the power to pursue the case with his own resources as he wished.

Baird watched Bender reaching for his cordless phone. His podgy face was dappled with the red mange that had festered there since his encounter with the bandits. It seemed to be spreading.

'That's a very nasty rash you've got there,' Baird said. 'You should really try and do something about that, Mr Bender.'

The American ignored him. As Baird left the room Bender's attention was on his phone call.

'What was the name of that kid with the bus company?' he was saying. 'The one with the flowers?'

Baird walked off up the long corridor, trying to keep his back straight.

Margot would help him. Things were boiling up, and the time had come.

It was a miserable grey morning. He had asked Mother to wake him early, and they all thought it was a job interview again. He had to put on his too-small jacket and Father's flowery tie, and Father asked him test questions over breakfast like, 'What is seven and a half of fourteen?' and 'Where is Patagonia?' Father thought a general education was the best asset a man could have.

He waited at the bus shelter in Princes Street, and managed to catch Margot coming off the third Newhaven bus. She was surprised and happy to see him there, on her way to work, and she waved and smiled even as she was coming down the steps of the bus. Then she gave him a hug and kissed him, but she seemed impatient when she saw how worried he was.

They walked along the road on the way to the bus station, and Margot was very quiet. It was hard to know where to start.

'His name's Nigel,' he said. 'I'm sure I saw something move in his beard.' Margot just looked straight ahead of her as she walked. She was weighing things up in her mind and deciding what should be done, he knew.

'He's just come out of Carstairs for the fifth time,' Will said. 'He said he was goin' tae bite Bruce's head off.'

Margot glanced at him for a second and shook her head with a wee smile. She could always see the funny side of things. But it was important and she really understood how he felt.

'But he's really like that,' Will said. 'He would! We're supposed to do this bus tomorrow, but it's all different.' He pulled his timetable out of his pocket and showed her the bus. 'The Strathalt run – with him.' A couple of early-morning shoppers stopped to peer at Will, and he realised he had been squeaking. Something funny had happened to his voice, and it came out sounding like a girl's. He coughed.

Margot peered at the timetable for a moment, and he put it away. She stopped walking and looked at him. It was beginning to rain.

'It's the Women's Institute outing,' she said. He hadn't known that. Margot spoke as if she was talking to a bairn who had lost his pet spider. 'Och it's a rotten business, Will, and you're better off out of it,' she said, nodding her head. They started walking again.

He was having trouble explaining, and he waved his arms in front of her. 'But I said I'd go,' he said. She gave him a very serious look as she walked. Was he squeaking again? He tried to speak deeply. 'They were all goin' on at me.'

Margot sniffed, and he noticed that she looked as if she felt even worse than he did. Mother would have packed her straight off to bed if she'd seen her.

'Think, Will,' she said after a while. She was nearly shouting. 'What about me?'

Will thought furiously. Nothing was impossible until you'd tried it. 'There isnae room on the bike. But maybe if we had a sidecar . . .'

Margot stopped again. The rain was getting heavier, and he realised she didn't have a raincoat. She watched him with rain dripping down her face. She had said – she had said it was a rotten business. Will's stomach felt upset, much worse than rumbling. It couldn't be right.

'It's not all rotten,' he said. 'You used to think it was great. That was half what was great about it.'

Slowly her pretty face wrinkled up as she stared at him, and she went white. She hated him. Margot stood and screamed.

'You're so stupid! You're so stupid! Can't you see how it's changed? You've changed and I've changed and Ronnie's changed! Will, do you not know I . . .'

She shook her head, turned round and started walking towards the bus station through the rain. He watched her, shaking.

'Margot!' he shouted. 'Don't go away, you're getting wet.' His legs began to move and he was running after her, pulling off his Camper's World £4.99 waterproof jacket. He caught her just outside the main entrance to the bus station, and plonked the jacket over her shoulders as she walked.

'Don't get wet, Margot,' he said, and walked off in the other direction. His stomach rumbled and his eyes hurt and his whole body was trembling, but he walked as briskly as he could, because he knew exactly where he was going.

He never noticed the white limousine pulling up outside the bus station and the crew-cut man ordering Margot to get in.

— 17 —

The police dragnet was tightening. It was in all the papers. There was even a rumour the Americans were running their own investigation, because so many American tourists had been done. There were plans to get helicopters patrolling over the mountains, and they were going to have plain-clothes policemen on a lot of the buses.

Ronnie wasn't worried. Conditions were changing in the combat zone, and quite simply the business would keep pace. You had to move with the times. There was no way Ronnie was going to become the Mr Hardwick of the crime world.

All the groundwork had been done. In less than twenty-four hours the new, expanded operation would swing into action, and the police wouldn't know what had hit them. Ronnie had learnt a lesson at Lochgoilhead, and next time they would be prepared to deal with trouble. Everything was ready. The only unaccountable thing in the whole set-up was Ronnie's legs. They had brought him to the cemetery.

That morning he had handed in his resignation to Mr Hardwick, collected several boxes of necessary stocks and carried them to the bedsit. Then he ran over the schedules for tomorrow, checked the equipment and filled up the bike. He had just walked out to take the air, and here he was.

Ronnie took a drag at his cigarette. The weather had cleared up since the morning, though the ground was still wet. He was all right, he was sitting in his coat. There wasn't anyone else around. Why should there be? There was no earthly reason why he should be there either.

He tried a smoke-ring. He hadn't said a word since he arrived, he was finished with all that. Even if there had been anybody to talk to, what was there to say? He had grown out of it.

He threw the cigarette down, and it sizzled out on the wet grass. He would go soon. Below him the gravestones ran down the slope and disappeared over the curve of the hill to the bottom. Why would anyone want to come to a dead place?

The top of a head came bobbing into view up the hill, and then the top of a face underneath it. It was Will Bryce's face. Ronnie had explicitly told him never to bother him in the cemetery, and here he was. He had probably forgotten altogether. Ronnie stared as more and more of Will came into sight over the edge of the hill. He was dressed like an idiot – a purple shirt and flared trousers and a jacket that was too small. Ronnie shook his head. It was so wearing.

Will came right up and sat down beside Ronnie on the wet grass, looking down the hill. Slowly Ronnie turned to him. Will had no business being there.

'I thought I told ye I'd pick ye up tomorrow,' Ronnie said.

Will said, 'I'm no' goin'.'

Just like that. What a dirty trick. Will was a pathetic character, he was like a soft Don Robertson. Ronnie didn't need someone like that.

'All right,' Ronnie said, busying himself with getting a cigarette out and lighting it.

'You'll need tae bring me the mask and the puffer,' he went on, blowing the smoke out of his nose. 'I'll see ye get your share o' the money. It's a different game now, ye're probly better off out of it.'

Will looked embarrassed, playing with his shoe-laces. He'd said what he came to say, why didn't he just scram? Will Bryce could never do a single thing without mucking about. Not even this.

Will turned round. 'What are ye goin' tae do tomorrow?' he said quietly.

He really didn't understand. 'We're goin' tae put the boot in,' Ronnie said, lying back against the stone. 'We're goin' tae get some status.'

Will coughed. 'It's the Women's Institute,' he said. He kneeled up on his hunkers, looking right into Ronnie's face. 'Look, Penicuik,' Will said. 'We could go into hiding in Penicuik. Naebody would find us. We could wear disguises tae go tae the shops.' He ran his hand over his chin. 'I could grow a beard quite soon.' He hesitated. 'Margot, she said "Don't ye know I . . .".'

So that was it. 'I'm not interested in your women,' Ronnie shouted. 'Ye just havnae got a clue, have ye?'

Will looked confused, sprawling back on the ground. Ronnie shifted round and pointed to the two gravestones. 'What does that say?'

Will read them. 'Brown,' he said. He quickly crawled over to one side and sat again, looking worried. He hadn't realised he'd been sitting on them.

'What's my name?' Ronnie said.

Will stared at him. 'Ronnie.' He paused, and Ronnie watched him. 'Ronnie Wotherspoon.'

'I don't know who's down there,' Ronnie said, pointing under him. 'I just picked them.' He stared at Will as if he was burning holes in him. 'See I havnae got people tae tie me down, pal. I'm goin' places, and I don't want any baggage with me. Right?'

Will stood up, trying to wipe the wet grass off his flared trousers. So that was that. Ronnie had grown sick of Will anyway. It was just his past. He watched Will shambling off down the hill.

Damn. Ronnie jumped. He'd forgotten about his cigarette, and it had burnt down to his finger. He dropped it in the wet grass, and wiped his finger on his coat. When he looked up, Will was standing in front of him, pointing at him.

'Jeely pieces!' Will shouted. Ronnie had never heard Will shout before. It was spooky. 'Thousands of jeely pieces,' Will shouted. His face was red, and his hand shook as he held it out, pointing. 'I kept you alive for more than a year while you were savin' up for that bike. Every day, pastin' up a sandwich and smugglin' it out the house for you.'

Will bent over, his eyes staring into Ronnie's face, still yelling. A spot of spit hit Ronnie on the cheek, and he moved backwards towards the stones. There was something frightening about it.

'And you don't have people to tie ye down,' Will shouted. 'And what about the clown and the wolfman? So what are ye now? You are a clown, a clown in a stupid big leather coat, an' who's goin' tae care when you an' that animal meet a couple of hard men that are bigger than you? Who's goin' tae care now?'

Ronnie watched as Will turned and walked away down the hill again. He saw him disappear among the stones going over the edge of the hill, and then reappear at the bottom, near the gate. No thoughts went through Ronnie's mind at all. He was so angry he thought he would burst. He stood up and ripped his leather coat from his shoulders, and slammed it on to the ground as hard as he could. Then he started running.

Will was just at the gate when Ronnie caught him. They walked side by side for a few steps, and Ronnie tried to smile.

'Ninety quid that coat cost me,' he said, wiping his eyes on his sleeve.

The Americans were talking among themselves, and Margot sat alone on the chair in the middle of the room, trying to dry up. She had cried a lot in the last few weeks, but it seemed to be an inexhaustible supply. Endless days and nights of pushing Will to think for himself, always hoping it wasn't too late, and of course it was. In little things he was the kindest person in the world, but big things only made him confused.

It was partly her fault. She had only started to look at the situation properly when she was hopelessly involved. It wasn't the sort of situation that could stand much looking into.

The fat piggy one was leaning against a table, looking through the timetable he had got from Will's rain-jacket. She knew tomorrow's bus was ringed in red felt pen. That was the way Ronnie always did it for Will.

'I'm going to be home in twenty-four hours,' she heard the fat one murmuring to himself. He wanted her to call him Fritz. She shuddered, wondering what his real name was. He had a horrid birthmark on his face, and he was always scratching at it.

He had slapped her bottom as they were coming into the bare basement room, but she hadn't told them anything, though they'd been at her for several hours.

She hardly needed to. After they forced her into the big white car they drove up St Andrew's Street, and the fat one flipped his thumb out the window and said, 'Friend of yours?' And there was Will, walking doggedly along in his shirt-sleeves through the rain. They couldn't know that he was one of the bandits, but the timetable in Margot's pocket had done the damage. All they had to do was be on that bus.

Margot hadn't had anything to eat or drink for five or six hours. She hadn't believed they were proper policemen until they had come to the police station. Why couldn't they at least be Scottish policemen?

One of the crew-cut ones passed her with two cups. 'Cup of coffee?' he said. Margot glared at him. Her eyes would be good and bloodshot by now, which would help the effect. 'Stick your head in a chanty,' she said.

Crew-cut put a cup on the table by Fritz and said, 'Shall I give Baird a call?'

Fritz threw the timetable down and took a sip of coffee. 'Forget it,' he said. 'This is my baby now.' He pulled a wallet out of his jacket, folded up the timetable and slipped it in as Margot watched. He had a colour photograph of a dog in a little window in his wallet.

He bent down with his hands on his knees so he could look into her face. 'Hey angel,' he said, smiling at her. 'How do you fancy going for a bus ride tomorrow, you and me?'

Margot couldn't help herself. Tears just poured out of her.

They took the bus to Wester Hailes to let Will pick up some stuff. On the way they talked more than they had done for ages, mostly about the old days when they were at school.

Will filled a tatty old suitcase with his clothes, and then he brought it through to the sitting-room and crammed his records into it. Ronnie helped him sit on the top while he did up the buckles. They were going on a new adventure.

'Do they have a bank in Penicuik?' Ronnie said.

Will gave him a look. It wasn't a very good joke. But Penicuik wasn't such a bad place, it had shops and houses and all sorts.

They would take a ration of the money, find somewhere to stay, and Will could work on his beard and they could make plans. It would be a breath of fresh air.

The front door slammed, and the sound of tuneless singing floated up the corridor. 'Love on the do – o – ole,' it went, 'lo – ove on the dole.' Isla came in, wearing several necklaces, bangles and rings all over her arms and hands, and a tiara on her head. She stood watching them, licking an ice-lolly. They ignored her.

Will spoke as he went through to the kitchen to get his dirty socks. 'Where's Mum?'

'Gone tae aerobics,' Isla said. She settled on the arm of the settee, staring at Ronnie. He smiled at her, but it didn't make any difference.

Will reappeared with an armful of dirty socks and started stuffing them through a hole in the side of the suitcase.

'Ye'll have tae tell her I've – gone tae New Mexico,' Will said. 'Tae work wi' Carol Paton's big brother. But I'll send a postcard.'

'Right,' said Isla. She was sucking the colour out of the ice-lolly, turning it into a clear block of ice.

'They've got Mary Harrison,' she said.

Will froze with his hand still inside the case.

'Who? Who's got her?'

'The pigs,' Isla said, sucking at her lolly. 'They picked her up in the street.' A big chunk of ice fell off the side of the stick, but she caught it in her ring-covered hand and flung it straight into her mouth. 'She won't crack,' she said, her mouth bulging. 'I know she won't crack.' She swallowed and began to saunter around the furniture as she spoke, talking to the room in general. 'Because if she cracks, I'll tell them about her and Bobby Martin.'

Will stuffed the last sock hurriedly into the case and jumped over it to the phone in the corner of the room. 'Right,' he said, 'just one call and then we'll get going.'

Ronnie stood and watched Will dialling, pleased. Will really seemed to know what he was doing. The robbery business had done wonders for him.

'Do you think ye've finished growin'?' It was Isla again, standing right beside Ronnie and sticking her lolly stick into her tiara. She was almost as tall as he was. Ronnie glared at her, and she sauntered out of the room, swinging her hips, smiling back at him.

He sat absent-mindedly polishing his glasses.

'Shit!' said Will, slamming down the phone. There was no answer at Margot's flat. He picked up the receiver again, dialling the bus station this time. Ronnie sat back down on the case. There were a lot of things he would miss in Penicuik.

'Strathalt,' Ronnie heard Will say. Will put the phone down, and looked very grimly at Ronnie. 'She's going to be on that bus,' he said.

After they had unpacked the case, Ronnie stayed for tea with Will's family. Most of Will's records were broken, but nobody said anything about it. Will's father went on for hours about the advantages of having a job like Ronnie's, and got a hell of a shock when Ronnie said he'd resigned. Ronnie didn't care.

Will and Ronnie stood out on the balcony before Ronnie left, watching the city lights. It was a fine evening, with a new moon shining on the tower blocks of the estate. They both hung over the concrete rail, staring out.

Will said, 'Ronnie, do ye want to come tomorrow?'

'Aye,' Ronnie said. He watched the moon for a minute. He was glad Will had decided what they should do. 'It's all finished now, isn't it?' he said.

'We're still going,' Will said. 'One more time, to Strathalt. The clown and the wolfman.'

It was late, and the floodlights on the distant castle were going out, one by one. Ronnie sighed. 'Funny business,' he said.

– 18 –

It was a remarkable break. An officer on the beat came across her, sitting on the kerb in a housing estate in the south west of the city.

She wore a green patterned mini-dress, and she had long

blonde hair. She was about five years old. The officer noticed she was playing with something in the gutter, and as he got nearer he could make it out. It was a string of pearls, flashing in the sun.

The usual procedure in a case involving a child was to go straight to the parents, but in this instance it was impossible. The child would not say who her parents were. In fact, she wouldn't say anything at all. In due course the pearls went for analysis at forensic and the child arrived for analysis in Baird's office at Headquarters, escorted by WPC Johnson.

They sat her on Baird's desk, and she gazed about the room with dark blue eyes and didn't say a word. WPC Johnson brought her a cup of hot chocolate, which she drank. In three hours she drank eleven cups of hot chocolate, and went to the bathroom five times, and by that time the report on the pearls had arrived. They had been stolen in July, from a Frenchwoman on a day-excursion bus. Estimated value: £1,250.

She was tough. The boys in the outside office came over all broody and trooped through to pinch her cheek and ask her when her birthday was. She didn't like that at all, but she didn't crack.

A dolled-up lassie from Social Services arrived to take the little girl away from the big nasty policemen. She knelt down and said in her sweetest talking-to-children voice, 'Would you like to go home now dear?' The kid gripped the edge of Baird's desk and started bawling. She wouldn't let go.

So Baird was stuck with her, for the moment at least. They tried introductions. Baird went slowly round the room. 'I'm James,' he said. 'And this is Margaret.' WPC Johnson simpered. Baird crossed the room. 'This is Donald –' Dunn waved – 'and this is Neil –' Harley pulled a funny face. Baird came to the telex machine. 'And this is Henry.' He crossed back to his desk, speaking very clearly. 'Now, who are you?'

The child looked at each of them in turn. She cleared her throat. 'Bo Derek,' she said.

Bender had disappeared downstairs to some office in the basement where they'd found room for him, and as far as Baird knew he hadn't been told about the child. Baird was determined not to let this break slip through his hands. He had children of his own, a chartered surveyor in Sheffield and a baker's wife in Aberdeen, and he knew he hadn't lost the knack. He sent Dunn out with a shopping list and a handful of expenses money.

Harley tried some more funny faces, crouching down by Baird's desk so his head was right in front of the child's. He had an unusual talent. He crossed his eyes, rolled them independently, and made them disappear till only the whites were visible. He waggled his ears, and made his hair move about on his head. He stuck his tongue out upside down, stretched his lower lip over the tip of his nose, and clacked his teeth to the tune of *Scotland the Brave*. The child didn't move a muscle.

Baird bent down beside Harley. Did Bo want to see all round police headquarters? She shook her head. Did Bo want to go for a ride in a police car? No. Did Bo want a free ticket to the policeman's ball?

'I dinnae like pigs,' she said. 'And ma name's Mary.'

Dunn arrived back just in time. Baird took the bag from him and peered inside. He could see Mary trying to peer as well. He dug around, and pulled out a family-size bar of chocolate. Mary's eyes followed every minute movement of the bar from Baird's hand to the top of his desk.

'Where did the pearls come from, Mary?' he said. She looked longingly at the chocolate, and then at Baird, and shook her head. He tried a tapestry set and a wind-up car, with the same results. Then he brought out Little Jackie. He could see Mary biting her lip, watching.

Little Jackie cost a week's expenses. Baird unwrapped her, and Harley and Dunn crowded round the desk. Mary stared and stared as they worked Little Jackie's blinking eyes, and Dunn read the box and discovered how to make Little Jackie wet her nappy. Mary sucked her finger.

They put Little Jackie on the floor of the office, and she shuffled along, whirring. Then Harley pulled the cord on her back, and a quavering little voice started to sing. 'Baa baa black sheep, have you any wool . . .' Harley and Dunn took up the chorus. 'Baa baa black sheep, have ye any wool . . .'

Mary turned to Baird and rubbed her eyes. 'Mary Harrison, 26a Tweedie Court, Wester Hailes. I want ma mum,' she said.

When Mr and Mrs Harrison arrived, Mary was asleep in Baird's chair. All Baird could do was wait till the morning and hope she told her parents. He had four men go out to Wester Hailes and start doorstepping – who she knew, who she played with, school friends and the like – but it would take time. Baird went home with Little Jackie on the back seat of his car and ate the bar of chocolate.

When morning came they were no further forward. Mary Harrison wasn't squealing. The Wester Hailes lads could turn up with the goods any minute, but Baird still felt uncomfortable. He didn't trust Bender. With his finicky obsession the American might just stumble on a fluke and finish Baird off once and for all.

Baird was playing with a box of fish-flies when the machine in the corner clanked and ground into life. He had had the option of early retirement, of course, but three years ago he saw no reason to take it. The life suited him, generally, until now.

'Message from Henry,' said Dunn, handing him the telex. Baird fished out his reading glasses and squinted at it. His eyes left the sheet of paper only once, when he glanced up for a second at the ringing of a telephone. It was Harley's phone, the blue one. Baird scanned the telex a second time.

It was astounding. Offensive. It was political interference at its most impractical and irresponsible. It was grossly unfair on Baird and his men. And he had no option but to act on it, immediately. The ball had been placed quite firmly in his hands. He stood up.

'Get Bender,' he called across to Dunn, waving the telex. 'Everything's changed.'

Dunn simply shrugged at him. 'He's gone,' he said. 'He left early this morning.'

Damnblast, thought Baird. Harley jumped out of his seat, waving excitedly with his free hand while he listened to the telephone. 'They're here!' Harley shouted, reaching for his jacket. 'They're right in the town!'

What a fuss. People were hooting their car horns and shouting, and waving their arms and flashing their lights. Will could see them out of the corner of his eye. He concentrated on looking straight in front of him, over Ronnie's shoulder.

The sun was shining on Calton Hill, up ahead. He brushed a strand of orange hair from Ronnie's mask away from his face. It was a busy morning on Princes Street, and though they weren't going very fast, Ronnie was travelling straight through any red lights.

The traffic was all jammed up with people looking at them, and the bike zipped along the narrow lane up the middle of the road. Drivers were leaning out of their car windows, cheering. At the bottom of the Mound a football fan unrolled a big Scottish flag and waved it at them. They shot past a traffic policeman, and Will noticed him staring, and getting out his pocket radio.

It was a fine sunny morning, though a cool breeze fluttered through the front of Will's mask.

'Nice weather for it,' Ronnie said.

Will looked at the sky. It was a clear, deep blue.

'Aye, I've seen worse,' he said.

It had been a brilliant dawn when they set off. They sped through the gleaming estate before many folk were about, and clanked along the tree-lined streets of the suburbs. They were in no hurry, and Ronnie took the bike on a long sweep round the outskirts of the city, past Redford Barracks where a squad of soldiers stopped marching to watch them go by. Then down through the Grassmarket and into the centre of town.

They turned off Princes Street up North Bridge and into the Old Town. There were fewer cars about here, and Ronnie opened up the throttle as they raced along the wide roads. At a crossroads a group of kids in school uniform and a lollypop man stood and pointed.

Then back eastwards along the banks of the canal, tearing

through clouds of steam that gushed from the tangle of pipes in the huge Central Brewery. Will could hear police sirens in the distance, and when he glanced back he noticed a huddle of blue and white flashing lights heading in their direction.

'Course it's nothin' like that really hot summer we had five years ago,' he said.

Ronnie didn't look round. 'Ye're never happy, are ye?' he said.

This time as they headed down towards the Grassmarket Ronnie steered the bike down a steep lane and on to Victoria Terrace, a pedestrian walkway built into the side of the tenement far above the main road. Will watched a police car shoot across the market, siren blaring and lights flashing. It raced up until it was running almost parallel to the bike, three stories down.

They reached George IV Bridge dead level, but the police car was hopelessly jammed in the traffic at the intersection. The bike flew across the pavement in front of it and down towards Princes Street. Up above them a crowd of workmen perched on scaffolding stopped what they were doing to shout and wave at the chase, banging noisy hammers on the hollow iron pipes.

This time on Princes Street the noise was twice as bad, and cars were clogged up all over the road. As the bike cruised past beneath the shadow of the castle, Will noticed that a number of the cars in the jam now were police cars, with policemen thumping angrily on the windows at them. The traffic policeman just stood and grinned as the bike came round him again. People were running out of the shops to jump and scream and cheer and chase after them.

'I think we've been this way before,' Will said.

'Lovely view of the castle,' said Ronnie.

They turned down through the New Town and clattered along the cobbled streets towards the coast, going as fast as they could. By the time they reached the Forth Bridge the roads behind seemed to be swarming with a clutter of police vehicles of all shapes and sizes, heading in their direction. They were getting closer all the time. Ronnie weaved the bike in and out of the cars on the bridge, gaining a few moments.

About the middle of the bridge the bike drew level with a gigantic articulated lorry, covered in pictures and stickers that said 'Supertrucker'. Will could see the lorry-driver grinning down at them. He was a wee guy with a moustache and grey hair. He winked, and pulled a handle, and the lorry made a noise like a foghorn going off.

As Ronnie accelerated away, Will looked back to see the lorry swerving across the road, backwards and forwards. It was slowing down, blocking all the police cars behind it. There was another great foghorn noise, now mixed with the dee-daws of the police cars, and the lorry-driver flashed his lights. They were getting a bit of leeway.

'Four years ago,' Ronnie said. 'It was four years ago, that really hot summer.'

He opened the throttle as far as it would go, and the bike sped northwards into the mountains.

It was hard to believe. They really had come into the middle of the city, in broad daylight, wearing their full ridiculous costumes, and paraded up and down in front of tens of thousands of people. Then they had gone right round in a circle and done it all over again.

Baird spent forty minutes sitting fuming in a stationary police car in Princes Street, so he had ample opportunity to study what it was they were doing. The town was a shambles, people had simply left their cars in the middle of the road and taken their binoculars to watch the show. Seventeen police cars were stuck around town, and Dunn only managed to get Baird's car out of it by driving along a crowded pavement for half a block. Somebody threw a tomato at the car, and Baird flinched as it hit the window. He watched it slowly sliding down in front of his face.

The people had just lost control. They were hanging out of windows, cheering and clapping the bandits as they went by, and booing the police cars. It wasn't just a few of them, either, it was everybody – shoppers, kids, business people – and tourists. Some of them tried to run to keep up with the motorbike, or pedalled furiously along on bicycles for several hundred yards. It was an unholy mess.

They couldn't escape, of course. There was no way a motorbike that size could outrun the law once it had been sighted. When Dunn had disentangled the car he turned northwards straight away, and pretty soon they had joined a posse of squad cars in pursuit of the robbers. Every so often on a straight stretch of road they could see them, their silly masks catching the sunlight in the distance.

At the Forth Bridge a drunken lorry-driver fouled things up, and they lost visual contact with the bike. They joined with the local force and split into three groups to follow the roads north into Fife, and within ten minutes they could see the bike again, fleeing ahead of them through the Perthshire foothills.

They followed it for half an hour, spotting it and catching up and then losing it again. Every time a police car got within about six hundred yards, the bike would dodge off the main road and travel cross-country. After a few minutes it reappeared on the road again. Baird had an uncomfortable feeling he was being led.

He wondered where Bender had got to. They had had some fine entertainment in the office that morning when Bender's lawyer rang long-distance. He came through on Dunn's phone, to say that the American had got his divorce, but there might still be problems. Bender, however, was nowhere to be found.

Ten miles from the Strathalt forest, Headquarters came on the line. Mary Harrison had broken down and confessed everything, and the search was on for a sixty-year-old man with slick-backed hair and a Hitler moustache, last seen catching a train to Aberdeen.

Baird cursed under his breath as the car entered the forest. The whole damn business was going to need a phenomenal amount of sorting-out.

Half a mile ahead, the bike had the road to itself. It raced headlong round a wide curve and straight into the path of a tour coach. Both bike and bus skidded to a halt, stopping just short of a collision.

There was a hiss as the door of the bus opened. Ronnie jumped off the bike a split second after Will, and heard it fall to the ground with a clatter behind him. Will was first up the steps.

'Margot!' he yelled. She was sitting in the courier's seat at the front, with her back turned to the door. She spun round to face them.

It was a man. A podgy man in a courier's uniform, with a horrible red mark across his face. He smiled nastily at Will and Ronnie. There was something familiar about him.

'Dear me,' Will said to the man. 'What are you wearin'?'

Ronnie was sure he had seen him somewhere before. He stretched his arm over Will's shoulder, pointing the puffer right in the man's face. 'Okay,' he said. 'Hold it.'

Still grinning, the man raised his right hand. He had a big black gun, and he aimed it at them. It looked like a real one. 'No, sunshine,' he drawled, 'you hold it.' He pressed a button on the dashboard, and the bus door slid shut.

There was a commotion at the back of the bus and people screaming, and Ronnie realised the place was packed with women. They all looked very respectable, middle-aged and eld-erly, with hats and dresses and handbags, and they were jittering about nervously in their seats, especially at the back. One old lady in the rear seat was going wild. She stood up and ripped off her hat and veil, and underneath she had a beard. Nigel. He swung out his sawn-off shotgun and aimed it up the aisle.

'No Jim,' he shouted. 'You hold it.'

The American's eyes fixed on Nigel for several seconds. It occurred to Ronnie that he might just be mad enough not to drop his gun. Women in hats shrank away and whimpered as Nigel lumbered up the aisle with a great toothless grin. His shotgun was pointing at the American's head, and his grin got wider as he raised the stock to rest against his shoulder. There was a thump as the American's gun hit the ground. His flabby face was quivering.

Nigel paused for a moment and leered out of the bus window. In the distance there was the noise of police sirens, and round the corner came a stream of cars, their lights flashing as they drew up to the bus. A man in a deerstalker hat stuck his head out the window of the lead car, holding a loudhailer. 'Okay,' he shouted. 'Everyone on the bus, hold it there.'

Cars and vans and bikes were crowding round in a circle on the grassy verges by the bus. Policemen ran about, taking up positions behind cars, aiming guns and watching through binoculars. Some of them wore riot gear and carried shields, others had bullet-proof jackets. Overhead, there was the chatter of a helicopter.

The inside of the bus was completely silent. Everybody was watching Nigel and Will and Ronnie. The American had crawled under the courier's seat, and had his arms over his head. Ronnie noticed Margot, sitting about five rows from the front in an aisle seat just beside where Nigel was standing. She was wrinkling her nose up, trying not to look conspicuous.

The man with the deerstalker stood behind his car, talking into the loudhailer over the roof. 'I want you to step off the bus one by one with your hands raised,' he said.

Slowly Nigel grinned, and he looked at Ronnie.

'Fight!' he said. He was having the time of his life. Ronnie pushed himself in front of Will, and Nigel turned to the passengers beside him and grabbed hold of Margot. He pulled her up, twisting her arm painfully behind her, and waded to the front of the bus with the shotgun barrel held to Margot's head. Ronnie could feel Will pushing sharply behind him, and he held him back.

'See me, I'm bullet-proof,' Nigel said to Ronnie. He glanced quickly out of the window. The police had all taken up position, and there was no movement outside.

'Right pal,' Nigel said. 'We'll take the bike. You get the boot intae as many pigs as ye can on the way. Nae mercy.'

'Let go,' Margot shouted. 'Let go! Take your hands off me!' She was really fighting now, hitting him with her free hand. Nigel didn't even seem to notice.

'Ronnie!' Will said, nearly pushing Ronnie over. 'Let me past!'

Nigel looked expectantly at Ronnie. Ronnie held the shotgun barrel away from Margot's head with his thumb and forefinger, and blasted Nigel in the face with the puffer. 'I'm sorry Nigel,' he said.

Nigel's grip on Margot loosened, and he shook his head. It was covered in white powder. Then his hands went to his face and he slowly crumpled up, groaning and wheezing and scratching at his full-length rose-pattern dress. There was a deafening shout, and a spasm ran through Nigel's body, shaking the bus. He was sneezing.

Will ran past Ronnie and caught Margot in a hug. All at once the respectable ladies with the hats burst into applause, clapping and clapping. Ronnie didn't know what to do. It was the Women's Institute. They were all smiling at him.

As Nigel lay twitching on the floor, the American got up from under the courier's seat and put his hand firmly on the shotgun Ronnie was holding.

'I'll take that, sucker,' he said.

The police moved very fast. Ronnie saw his bike being loaded into the back of a van, and two policemen dragged Nigel, still grunting and spluttering, out of the bus and into the back of a police car. The car drove off. The American threw off his courier's jacket, and a man with a crew-cut gave him an ordinary suit-jacket. They searched Will, Margot and Ronnie, and then walked them across the road towards the van with the motorbike inside. None of them spoke.

They passed the old man in the deerstalker, who was directing operations outside. There were policemen everywhere, taking photographs of the bus, measuring distances, chattering to each other, and helping the women in the hats off the bus. The American grinned and said, 'What took you so long, Scotty?' as they went by, but the old man ignored him.

The van had no windows. It was just a box with a wooden bench on either side. The American hustled Will, Margot and Ronnie in, and then stood looking at them, smiling. They looked back. It was very cramped, sitting inside with the motorbike.

'Course what I worry about is what are mummy and daddy going to say?' the American said. Ronnie felt Will give a little twitch beside him. The American's face went very nasty. 'Now take those masks off,' he said.

Ronnie and Will looked at each other, and Will reached for his mask.

'I think you'd better read this.' It was the old man, standing beside the American. He didn't look as if he liked him. He handed him a folded sheet of paper, and the American started to read it.

The passengers were swarming around outside the bus. A few of them spread rugs on the grass among the police cars at the side of the road, and they passed around cups of tea from a big thermos flask. Several of the policemen were talking to them, writing things down, and sharing sandwiches from a hamper that had appeared on one of the rugs. Ronnie watched. It was quiet inside the van.

The American's face looked puzzled as he read the sheet of paper, and he pawed at the mark on his face. Ronnie wished he could remember where he had seen him before.

'You'll have some questions to answer about what you were doing with that gun,' the old man said, taking the sheet of paper gently out of the American's hands. The American just stood there, lost.

The old man started to shut the doors of the van. 'Also,' he said to the American, 'your lawyer rang to say the dog's yours. He says he'll ring if there's a problem.'

The second door closed, and Ronnie heard bolts being fastened outside. Most of the police cars were leaving, and he counted the car engines starting up and fading into the distance. After seven there was a rumble and a slight shaking inside the van, and they were moving.

Bender stood scratching his face in the middle of the road, watching the top-security van drive off and disappear into the hills. He felt dazed. One by one the vehicles dispersed, and the tour coach started up and drove off.

There was the electronic wail of a cordless telephone ringing.

It was very gloomy inside the van. A small light-bulb glowed faintly in the ceiling, making long shadows across the three of them.

Once they had started, Ronnie took off his mask, and then Will did the same. There was no reason not to, at this stage. They sat in silence, though Margot kept rubbing at her eyes. What was there to say? They had known this was what they were coming to.

The van had terrible suspension, and they bounced up and down on the hard wooden benches as it went. Will and Ronnie were sitting on one side of the motorbike, and Margot was on the other, staring at Will. She had a little smile, as if she was pleased with what Will had done, but her face was all wet.

They wouldn't put her in prison. She might get probation or something, but it was better than what might have happened if she'd found herself alone on the bus with Nigel and his shotgun.

What did Ronnie have to lose anyway? It had been worth it just to have the last run through Edinburgh and up to the Highlands. It would be like going back to the home. Free bed and board, and education now as well, you could do exams and get qualifications in a place like that.

When they got a lawyer Ronnie would have to apply for a patent on the puffer as quickly as possible. The police might find it was just the thing for the man on the beat, and they could use bigger versions for mob violence at football matches and stuff like that. He could imagine them getting excited as they studied it through a microscope in the police laboratories. He might make a fortune.

Will pulled out his little golden brooch and handed it across the motorbike to Margot.

'I wanted you to have this,' he said. Margot looked at it, wiping her eyes. Something caught her attention, and she held it up to the dim light in the ceiling, and stared at it very closely.

'That's not gold,' she said to Will. 'It's not gold.' She really was pretty. She turned to Ronnie now, holding it up for him to see. 'It was meant to be gold, for his warts,' she said.

Ronnie had forgotten. He nodded. 'Aye.'

They were thrown to the side as the van did a sharp turn, and then there was a bump and it stopped. Ronnie heard a bang as somebody got out of the driver's door. There was a rattling and the sound of bolts being drawn at the back. He realised Margot and Will were kissing, leaning towards each other over his motorbike. He looked back at the van doors. This was it.

There was a crack of light, and one of the doors slowly opened. Ronnie's eyes took a moment to adjust to the big square of brightness. He rubbed them. All he could see was blue sky, and sea.

The old man had brought them to the edge of the world. He held his hand out to help Margot climb down, and Will and Ronnie jumped out after. They stood at the edge of the cliff, looking down. It must have been eighty feet sheer, and at the bottom there were jagged rocks where huge waves splashed and foamed.

Ronnie didn't like it very much. Will was worse, he hated heights, and he stood with his eyes shut, holding on to Margot. They were very near the edge. There was a spooky whistling from the wind, and the screams of a seagull, and the distant crash of the waves on the rocks.

The old man stood looking at them for a long time before he said anything. He didn't look such a bad old man. He was all tweeds and deerstalker and beard, like a gamekeeper that had gone into the police by mistake. But he'd obviously got out the wrong side of bed that morning. He just stood, staring at them while the wind whipped through their hair. If he went for them Ronnie was going to dive to the ground and hold on to the grass, trying to grab Will and Margot as he dived.

Eventually the old man took a sheet of paper from his inside jacket pocket. It looked like the same sheet he had shown to the American. Then he pulled out a pair of glasses and fitted them carefully to his face. Ronnie shivered. It was cold, with the wind tearing across the cliff. Will still had his eyes tight shut.

'This is a telex,' the old man said in a loud voice. He waited, staring, until Will opened one eye to look at it. 'A telex, from the Secretary of State for Scotland. He says –' the old man squinted at the paper – 'tourist spending is fifteen percent up since these activities started.'

The old man tugged at his beard and rubbed the back of his neck. He wasn't enjoying himself. The wind fluttered at the paper in his hand. Ronnie didn't quite understand. The old man read on. 'Bigger than the Loch Ness Monster,' he said. He looked up from the telex, and let his hand fall to his side. He shook his head, glaring at Will and Ronnie. He was very angry. 'Grossly irresponsible criminal behaviour of the most flagrant kind,' he said, staring really hard at them. Will's eyes were shut again, and his face was all screwed tightly up. Ronnie looked down, embarrassed. The wind was hurting his ears.

When he looked up the old man was reading from the paper again. 'Low profile, the Secretary says. Handle with the utmost discretion. Political hot potato.' He spat the words out. Ronnie wished he understood better. Why potato?

He watched the old man scrumple up the paper into a small ball, squeeze it really hard, and toss it over the edge of the cliff. The wind caught it and it flew out over the sea before tumbling down on to the rocks below.

The old man stood and stared again, his hands on his hips. He shook his head. 'Well I cannae let you go.'

– 20 –

The reporter stood on the edge of a cliff, his thinning hair blown about wildly by the wind. He gripped a big microphone, and clutched a sheaf of fluttering papers to his side as he talked, looking very gravely into the camera.

'And so it was here, in a last desperate bid to escape the tightening grip of the law, that the Highland heroes plunged to their deaths in the stormy seas below.'

The picture changed to a view of the side of the cliff. The camera panned down the craggy face, a good fifty-foot drop, and came to rest at the bottom. It zoomed in to a close-up of foaming waves smashing into bits of crumpled metal, including a wheel.

'Oh Mary,' Father said. He was devastated. The reporter talked on.

'All that remains is the battered wreckage of the Japanese motorcycle which carried them on so many daring raids, now strewn across the jagged rocks.'

'Oh my God,' Father said. He was slumped nearly horizontal on the settee, gawking miserably at the television in the corner. An empty can of beer sat on the coffee-table in front of him. He shook his head. 'Oh dear,' he said. 'Oh dear oh dear oh dear.'

Mother fussed briskly over the potted plants in the corner of the room. She had a small sprayer and two dusters, and she was dusting each leaf of the Cheese Plant, spraying it, and then polishing. 'Oh this is terrible,' she said.

Father nodded, still watching the screen. They were showing pictures of the clown and the wolfman on the motorcycle. The film was very out of focus and wobbly, and sometimes the camera would swing round to show a police car, with two policemen shouting and making obscene gestures. 'Courtesy of Japanese Television', it said underneath.

'I can hardly believe it,' Father said. 'I never thought it would end like this. They were so –'

'So frustrating,' Mother said, respraying a difficult leaf, 'trying to keep the whitefly off through a summer like that.'

Father hadn't heard. 'They won't be forgotten, ye know,' he said. He stretched his arm out to the table and tried to take a drink from the empty can. 'Legends never die. They never die.'

Isla thudded up the hall and appeared in the doorway, wearing her new dungarees. She surveyed the scene and sidled up to Mother, watching her burnish a leaf.

'Mum,' she said sweetly, 'can I move into Will's room now?'

Mother put the duster down and sighed. She missed Will. The house seemed quieter without him, although he'd never been a noisy child. But there was no point in everybody getting upset.

'You'll need to see what your father says, dear,' she said.

Father twisted his head round to squint over the back of the settee. Somewhere inside his head a small alert signal had sounded.

'Eh?' he said.

A man was killed by a potato in America.

Will had read about it in the paper. A restaurant chef in New York had thrown a rotten potato out of the kitchen window in a fit of temper. Sixty-three stories below, the man was taking his dog for a walk, and he was killed instantly.

It was really the last place Will wanted to be, even though everyone said New Mexico wasn't New York. Margot said make the most of it and bought sun-tan oil and Ronnie said be a man of the world, but it was no good. Even the food was different. It was hot like curries, and people drank tea with ice in it.

They sat in the Back Porch Bar most days, because there was a telly on the wall and sometimes they had stuff about the clown and the wolfman on. Will liked to see it, with pictures of the Highlands and Edinburgh, though it made him feel worse afterwards.

Alice didn't mind them sitting there. She ran the bar and she liked Scottish people. She said she had a grandfather who was Scottish, and she was always asking if they had ever heard of him. She let Ronnie bring Bruce too. Bruce hadn't enjoyed flying any more than Will, and he'd been sick in Ronnie's pocket. Will knew Bruce wanted to go home as well. He kept remaking his bed in different parts of the cage, every day. Nothing seemed right, abroad.

Even Margot was quiet. Sometimes she tried to get Will and

Ronnie to go on expeditions to the mountains or places where they had Red Indians, but she wasn't really enthusiastic.

One afternoon they were in the Back Porch and there was a half-hour programme on the clown and the wolfman. They had an American reporter telling the story, and there were pictures of Princes Street.

'Only that morning, thousands of shoppers in the city's main street witnessed the pair's greatest feat of daring as they roared through the capital without any pretence at furtiveness.'

Even Ronnie had got tired of the telly stuff now, but it was nice seeing home.

'Onlookers burst into wild cheering as the unforgettable figures of the clown and the wolfman sped past the rush-hour traffic. Little could they imagine the dramatic fate which awaited the outlaws.'

Ronnie took a good gulp of his latest sample. There was a whole shelf of drinks of different colours behind the bar, and Ronnie had decided he was going to try them all. He was on the yellows. He set the glass down and smacked his lips.

'Aye, it's good stuff that,' he said. 'Ye should try some. Tastes like gobstoppers.'

He was still wearing his jeans and leather jacket, although it was really hot. They were part of his character. Margot had made Will buy a pair of baggy shorts and a flowery shirt, and he didn't like them at all.

Will peered at his lemonade. There was something funny happening in it. He held it up to the light. 'There's bits droppin' off,' he said. 'There's bits comin' off my ice. There could be a germ in there. I read that –'

'Oh don't be such a big lassie,' Margot said without looking up. She was busy writing postcards.

'Aye,' Ronnie said importantly, taking another swig of the

yellow liquid. 'A germ or two never did anybody any harm. We're bigger than germs now, you and me.'

Margot passed Will a postcard. It had a picture of Albuquerque Municipal Building on the front, and printed on the back was 'New Mexico – Land of Opportunity'. She had addressed it to Will's parents, and had written 'Weather very nice' on it.

'Put your name on it,' she said to Will. He stared at her. 'They're your parents,' she said, getting annoyed.

Will looked round the bar and then at Ronnie, who was watching him doubtfully. The pictures on the telly were of the Highland roads now, and Strathalt. He wished they were home.

'They're very hospitable people here,' Ronnie said. 'Very good to tourists.'

Will had already written to Mother and Father to say he was doing a good job and making lots of money and had to get up early every morning. He didn't know what else to write.

'Do you think we'll ever be able tae go home?' he said to Ronnie.

Ronnie looked out the open door behind him. There was a Greyhound bus drawing up outside to pick up passengers. Ronnie looked back at Will with a smile, but he didn't say anything. The reporter on the telly was still at it.

'And all that remains, this sad, sodden reminder of mortality.'

He was standing at the edge of the cliff now, holding up the wolfman mask. It was all soaked and dripping on the reporter's suit.

Will tried to concentrate on what Ronnie meant. He was worried. When they'd killed the clown and wolfman at the cliff, the old policeman with the beard said he'd track them to the ends of the earth if he ever heard of them again. 'Ye've got tae have some respect for the dead, Ronnie,' he said. Ronnie leaned over to feed a nut to Bruce in his new cage as the reporter went on.

'We may never know who they were. But one thing is certain. No one can tame them now. The end of the story? Or the beginning of the legend? Melvyn Hamner, AM News Magazine, Scotland.'

Ronnie leaned seriously across the table to Will. 'Look,' he said. 'Do you believe in ghosts?'

— 21 —

BASHER BOWS OUT!

Super-Scot crimebuster James 'Basher' Baird, who only six months ago stunned the underworld by snaring the notorious Highland Highwaymen, retired yesterday aged sixty-five. Superintendent Baird, one of the Scottish police force's most outspoken and respected characters, plans to move to Perthshire.

'I am looking forward to a little peace and quiet at last,' he joked yesterday.

Superintendent Baird has rarely been out of the headlines for long in a distinguished career spanning forty years. Born the son of a debt-collector in Dunfermline, he was educated at Harold Laing Comprehensive, and left school to work in estate management before joining the Argyll and Sutherland Highlanders at the outbreak of war.

During an outstanding military career in North Africa and Europe he rose to the rank of Captain, and was awarded the DSC for bravery beyond the call of duty at Tobruk.

On returning to Scotland in 1946 he joined the Lothian and Borders Police in Edinburgh, where he has stayed ever since.

'I couldn't think of anything better to do,' he joked yesterday.

Superintendent Baird rose quickly through the police ranks, acquiring the nickname 'Basher' because of his no-nonsense approach to the violent core of organised crime in Central Scotland at the time. It was 'Basher' Baird who smashed the 'Red Ramsay' drugs ring in the mid-sixties, bringing about the conviction of twenty-three men for offences ranging from assault to supplying hard drugs.

In 1971 the Superintendent became a celebrity when he brought in multiple-murderer Harry Niven, the leader of Glasgow's most infamous gang of 'hard men'. Superintendent Baird pursued Niven across Scotland, finally cornering him in a Caithness farmhouse, where he persuaded him to give himself up. Niven, who subsequently spent three weeks in hospital, made persistent allegations of 'police brutality'. He was sentenced to life imprisonment.

But 'Basher' Baird's most memorable case must be that of the Highland Highwaymen, the infamous armed robbers who terrorised countless thousands of innocent tourists travelling by bus through the Highlands. Superintendent Baird formed the crack team behind 'Operation Bandit', the international investigation which finally tracked the robbers down to a Highland forest.

When the ruthless criminals escaped from the top-security van bringing them back to justice, it was Superintendent Baird himself who single-handedly pursued them to the Argyll coast and their watery grave.

'They just drove their motorbike straight for the cliff-edge,' he said at the time. 'I tried to stop them, but there was nothing I could do.'

Mr Baird has two children, James, a chartered surveyor, and Sandra, a housewife. His wife Margaret died in 1978.

A keen fisherman, he plans to devote himself to his hobby. 'Yes, I suppose I've still got something to catch,' he joked yesterday.

Pictured left to right: Chief Constable Alan Whitworth; Det. Sgt. Donald Dunn; Supt. James Baird; Det. Sgt. Neil Harley; a policewoman. The Chief Constable presented Supt. Baird with a silver model of a police car.

The days went by quite happily. Baird had a cottage, half a mile from the river, and it felt like home.

There was plenty to do. Wood to be chopped for the fire, tackle prepared, the cottage looked after. It was just a butt and ben, but he whitewashed the outside and fixed the gutters and the windows, and it was all he could ask for.

In the evenings he would sit by the fire, reading from his library, or maybe walk into the village for a couple of pints. He'd been coming here for years, and there was always a friendly face to talk to, if he felt like it.

As the months passed, he had the vaguest sense of missing the work. A publisher wanted him to write his memoirs, but he'd never been a great hand at the words, and in the end he declined.

There was too much the sense of looking back, as if the important things were all behind him.

Once a month he took the car into Edinburgh to stock up with building supplies or clothes or equipment from the tackle shop. He was striding down Princes Street one spring afternoon, and he stopped in his tracks, smitten by the strangest sensation. It was a face, a flat, round sort of face with glasses, nipping past him and round the corner. He felt as if he'd been visited by a spirit of the past.

After a while he found he hardly needed to venture into the city. His old haunts seemed different since he had left them, and everything he required for his life now was right on his doorstep.

He had a lot of success that summer with a new fly. It was a combination of old elements, a novel twist and the results of some serious experimenting the previous year. It worked like a dream. After it pulled in the third twenty-pounder he christened it the Basher Special. There were a few folk anxious to know the secret, but he could get a little jealous about his personal tricks of the trade.

It was a beautiful summer. Too hot for the fish, but he'd tramp out to the river with his sandwiches anyway and do some casting. There was still a part of him that kept an interest in the world of events, and it was his habit to take the radio with him for the one o'clock news.

He'd just had his sandwiches and switched on when he had a tug on the line. It was a Basher Special, but he couldn't believe it. It felt like a thirty-pounder. Unheard of for midday at that time of year.

He waded carefully out, his arms tightening with years of experience as he played the fish. The radio report which crackled distantly on the shore reached only some dim corner of his subconscious. With a silver flash the fish jumped, twisting in the air on the line before thrashing back into the water. Baird gasped in triumph. It was a huge beauty. He never lost the thrill.

The radio announcer's voice floated unnoticed over the river, mingling with the music of the water.

'American tourists visiting the Loch Ness area of Scotland yesterday reported a bizarre sighting at the lochside. They claimed to have seen the legendary Highland Highwaymen, the outlandish motorcycle bandits who plunged to their deaths from an Argyll cliff following a series of dramatic coach hold-ups several years ago. Tour guide Anne Nichols said, "It was a very hot day, and really visibility in the area was too poor for anyone to say with any certainty what it was they saw." One of the tourists, Mrs Esther Tapley of Kingston, Maine, said, "This has never happened to me before . . ."'